BEYOND THE MASK

BEYOND

THE GRASSLAND TRILOGY

THE MASK

DAVID WARD

AMULET BOOKS
NEW YORK

Library of Congress Cataloging-in-Publication Data

Ward, David, 1967–
Beyond the mask / by David Ward.
p. cm. — (The Grassland trilogy; bk. 3)
Summary: Having left the harsh life in Grassland and finally returned to her home and her father, Pippa and her friends must then go back to the land where they were slaves and try to forge a peaceful settlement with the Spears in order to avert tragedy for their village.
ISBN 978-0-8109-8345-8
[1. Slavery—Fiction. 2. Science fiction.] I. Title.

PZ7.W1873Bey 2009
[Fic]—dc22
2008024687

Text copyright © 2003 David Ward
First published by Scholastic Canada Ltd.
Map by Paul Heersink/Paperglyphs

Book design by Chad W. Beckerman

Printed and bound in U.S.A.
10 9 8 7 6 5 4 3 2 1

Amulet Books are available at special discounts when purchased in quantity for premiums and promotions as well as fundraising or educational use. Special editions can also be created to specification. For details, contact specialmarkets@abramsbooks.com or the address below.

ABRAMS
THE ART OF BOOKS SINCE 1949
115 West 18th Street
New York, NY 10011
www.abramsbooks.com

For Tess

Special thanks to
Ron Jobe, Tracy Zuber,
Scott Treimel, and
Sandy Bogart Johnston.

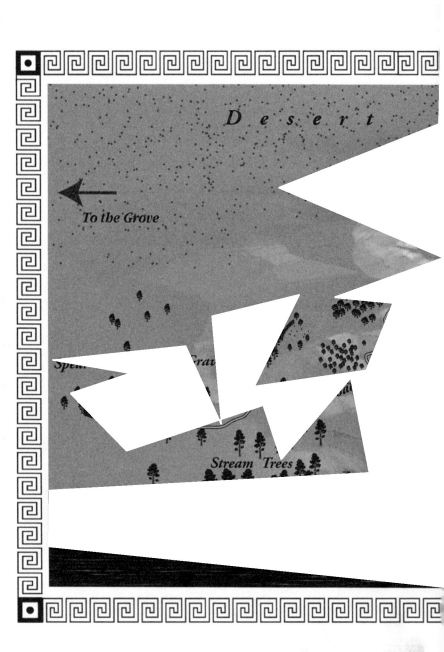

D e s e r t

To the Grove

Spea   Grav

Stream Trees

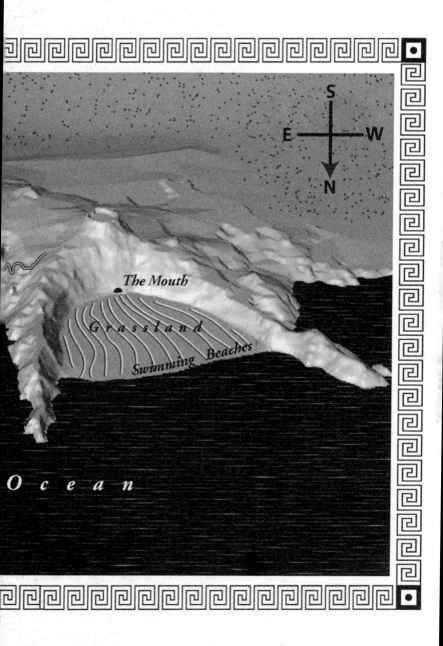

BEYOND THE MASK

I

THE RAIDERS CAME ON HORSE-
back. No less than twenty mounts trotted through the sparse
trees and meadow, making their way to the unsuspecting
village below. All were seasoned warriors—their war cloaks
were stained by water and sun, blood and time, and blended
with the dark woods on either side of them. There was not a
common helmet on their heads, but rather a foul collection
taken from the fallen in past battles. It was the way of a
reckless, merciless army. It was the way of Outside.

"We come too late," Thief whispered. "This will be a
slaughter. We should leave." He held a hand in front of his
mouth to hide his cloudy breath. It was cold in this land.
Colder than Pippa had said.

I stuffed my numb hands deep into my cloak. Thief's words rang ominously, but I didn't answer. Pippa had brought us here without disaster and I would not go against her wishes so quickly. Not after coming so far. So long.

Her eyes watched the rough column of soldiers. "There is time enough to warn the village," she said.

I weighed the distance between the first horses and the final slope. Dawn's pale light breaking across the water, coupled with a half moon, lit the way for the riders. "Not much time, Pippa. There are ten of us, on foot. If we hurry we might be able to warn the villagers enough that they can defend themselves. But not to escape. There is little place to hide down there from men on horseback." Dark green trees, taller than any we had seen in Grassland, kept us hidden. A fog rolled in from the sea and rested above the near fields like hearth smoke. I pursed my lips. It *was* a cold place, with dampness everywhere, and yet alive with greenness and fresh earth. I was thankful for the warm cloaks we had found in the boat that had carried us here.

Pippa followed my gaze. The village was small. No more than ten dwellings, nestled between the mountains and the sea. The homes clustered around a central path, with trees on either side hedging the village like cupped hands around a bowl. There were farms as well, but these were cleverly cut into the steep sides of the mountains like steps, difficult to get to, and spaced large distances apart. The easiest catch was the village, where there was food, water, and whatever other spoils the raiders could drag away with them.

I lifted Pippa's chin. "Do you wish us to risk everything for a village you are not even certain is your own?"

Her eyes, so green, stared back with the confidence of a soldier. "Do you need to ask?"

A warm brown hand rested on my shoulder and Feelah knelt beside us. "Coriko. Why do we all have to go? Why not just two? The little ones do not need to see another battle. You and my Thief go. Yell and make noise, then run for the woods. You will be gone before the raiders arrive, and everyone will be up with whatever weapons they have." She shrugged. "Then at least we have done what we can."

Pippa raised her eyebrows. Thief nodded. I turned my attention to where Bran watched over the little ones. It

3

was difficult for him not to be discussing plans. He was even getting better at speaking the language that united the rest of us: the language of warriors and slaves, the language of the Spears who had so long held us in thrall. How long ago that was. Spring and summer had passed. Winter, in all its bitterness, had kept us from exploring any farther north, and our days were spent seeking warmth.

For over three seasons we had been in this country, searching in vain for the village that Pippa had been taken from when the Spears stole her and brought her to Grassland. Pippa was constantly remembering more: names of places, lakes, mountains. But they were like a map drawn by a child—confused and with no understanding of distance.

I looked at my companions. We were a tired, ragged-looking company. Our clothes, soaked by the sea, bleached by the sun, and beaten by the winter, were ill-fitting at best. The boat we had taken from Grassland seemed to grow smaller each day. I despised even looking at it anymore.

Bran watched me with a furrowed brow. I signaled,

Come. Keeping low, he scrambled to my side. "What will we do?" He used the Northern tongue—a language, I realized, that the people sleeping in the village below us might use.

"Feelah says two go down to warn the village. The rest stay here. I doubt the raiders will enter the woods, so you should be safe here. There is a direct path through the meadow to the fjord."

His eyes narrowed. "You mean *three* of us go down."

I grunted. "If one of the little ones cries, or scouts are sent to the trees, we need you to be *here*. You must take them into thicker woods or back into the boat. And you have no skill with a sword yet. You would just as likely cut *me* down as one of the raiders!"

Pippa interrupted us. "This is my village. At least, with all my heart I believe it is. Do you see that last building? The one closest to the sea?"

I nodded. "Past the village, beyond the rise?"

"Yes. I have seen it before—I am sure of it." She took a deep breath. "Feelah's words are good. Not all should be in danger because of me. Coriko and I must go."

"I do not like it," Thief growled. "We have been in

5

danger before. And this is not the first village we thought was Pippa's. This is no different than any others. Coriko and I should go. There may be fighting."

Pippa slapped the ground. "This is the village. I know it!"

Thief and I exchanged glances. I could not remember the number of times we had crawled through fields or crept into towns all along this coast, only to discover that we had not found Pippa's home. And we could not ask what it was called, since her memory of the name had left her. It was a name she knew she would remember if she *heard* it, but that was no help to us now.

When the number of our days since leaving Grassland passed one hundred and fifty, I stopped hoping in names, and trusted only in letting Pippa see as many villages as we could. She would have to see it, and yet there seemed no end of little towns along this coast. Summer had turned to fall and then winter, and still we had not found it.

Even Bran had played his part, melting in with the children of strange villages to ask questions or to steal food. We learned more at every place, but our landings were becoming dangerous. The little ones were hard to

6

keep quiet and even harder to keep fed. We needed a regular supply of food to lessen the risk of being caught. My hunting skills with a bow and arrow had grown strong, but there were days when no living thing showed a whisker or feather. Worst of all, Bran had returned with horrifying news at the last port: a ship with an orange sail had anchored in the bay and sent a small boat to the town. Bran had learned that black-cloaked warriors were seeking a group of youths, two boys skillful with swords, and two girls, one with dark hair, the other with hair like the sun. They were giving coins to anyone who had information. I trembled at the thought of the Spears finding us and taking us back to Grassland. It was also confusing to hear of Spears openly landing in an area they had raided before, though we knew that they traded their shards as well. Were they becoming less warlike, as Pippa hoped? I doubted it.

Nudging Pippa, I whispered, "Thief is right. Let us go down. This is no place for pretty-colored dresses. It is probably not your village. Why should we risk everything? If the Spears have sent ships to find us, that can only mean that Marumuk has changed his mind about letting us leave."

"We don't *know* that that's why Spear ships are looking for us," Pippa countered.

Thief pulled a face. "Marumuk has not sent them to bring us presents! He is angry he let us go. Maybe he no longer listens to Tia's advice. Marumuk fears we will give away the secrets of Grassland."

I knew more than anyone that my former master was angry with us. He had shown that disappointment the last time we confronted each other in the tunnels beneath Grassland's mountain. And yet the powerful Marumuk—the greatest leader the Spears had ever known—had been persuaded to let us go. Even after spending all those months training Thief and me, and choosing us for his raiding parties. No, Marumuk's secrets were safe. I could not imagine why he searched for us now.

"This *is* the village," Pippa argued. "This is *my* village. And the people are in danger."

"We waste time," Thief warned. "Look! The raiders have made it halfway up the slope."

Already the raiders had picked their way through the thinning trees and were urging their horses into a trot. The mist clung to the horses' feet as if they were riding on clouds.

"Shut up, both of you!" Feelah commanded. "Listen to Pippa and go! Now!" She pulled hard on my braid, lifting me from the cold earth.

Grabbing Pippa, I pulled her deeper into the trees, calling quietly over my shoulder, "Stay here. Wait for us. We will come back with news. Keep the little ones safe."

"You be wise, Coriko!" Feelah called back.

The horses in the meadow had the advantage of short grass and bracken and little else to slow their passage. Pippa and I thrust branches from our faces, avoiding the sharp fingers of trees and the uneven soil where roots rose to trip us. The scent of earth filled the air and rain-laden boughs soaked our clothes.

"Faster, Pippa!" I gasped. The sound of jingling harness joined the pounding of our feet.

"I am trying!" Her words heaved with each breath. "I have not trained to be a soldier, as you have."

"Run!"

It was difficult to move freely with the burden of our cloaks. If it had not been so cold I would have shed mine

9

long before. As it was, Pippa's legs kept getting tangled in hers.

I was not worried about being caught while we remained in the woods. The soldiers were after the village and would not waste time chasing children through trees. The danger would be when we came out into the open. It was never wise to flout an army when they were close enough to strike us. As we scrambled down the steep slope toward the village, the trees began to thin. Soon there were few branches in our way and we moved faster through the low forest scrub. We passed a stack of piled wood and a cow grazing at the forest's edge.

"Farm," Pippa panted. Breaking through a final line of trees, we sped through a field of high grass, the uneven ground swishing noisily with our passing. A low stone wall appeared.

"Over it!" I yelled. There was no more need for silence. The earlier the townspeople woke, the better. The back of my foot nicked the top stone as I hurtled over, but I did not falter. Beyond the wall was a house with a thatched roof, still dark and asleep.

"Corki!"

I scrambled to a stop.

Pippa was caught on the wall by the bottom of her cloak, hooked firmly on a jutting stone. My knife was in my hand before I reached her. With a single stroke the cloak came free, leaving a patch of cloth stuck to the wall.

"Look there!"

Riders were streaming over the top of the hill and pouring down the slope in a waterfall of horses.

"We're too late!" I groaned. "We must go back, Pippa."

"Not yet." She pulled on my hand and we set off running even faster than before. Torchlight flickered in the farmhouse as we passed, and a shadow played at the window.

"Raiders!" I yelled. "Get up! Wake!"

The shadow disappeared and I heard the door open. Shouts broke out.

"The road, Corki," Pippa gasped. "We must take the road."

"They will catch us for certain if we do that! We will not even make it to the first home we reach."

"Yes we will!"

Our feet flew along the road. Hoofbeats sounded behind us, painfully close. Horses thundered along the road, gaining far more quickly than I liked. "They are charging," I panted.

"Almost there!" Pippa cried. A roughly hewn gate barred the way, twenty strides ahead of us. The wooden poles, made to keep animals within the village, were easy to clamber through. I hoped the gate would make the raiders pause before they smashed it down. The road disappeared and flowed into several muddy paths, most of which led to a string of dwellings. I heard the ocean crashing ahead and smelled salt in the air.

"What now?" I cried.

The village lay in stillness, hardly prepared for the doom about to break down their gate.

Pippa looked about helplessly.

"Get up!" I yelled into the silence. "Wake! Wake!"

There was no response for a moment. Finally a sleepy voice mumbled something from the nearest door.

"*Wake!*" Pippa and I yelled together. We ran to the house and pounded with our fists. I faced the gate. Despite the dampness, a dust cloud, stirred by twenty horses, announced the raiders' coming.

"Pippa, we must leave now! Back to the forest. We have done enough."

Her eyes were wide, yet she stood her ground. "No! There are people here, Coriko. Perhaps children, women, old ones. They deserve—"

A man bolted into the street, dressed only in breeches, swinging a large stick.

"Who are you?" His accent, although thick, was familiar. "You'll get no free food here! Be gone before it's truly light."

"Behind you!" Pippa pointed to the soldiers riding toward us.

"Raiders!" the man screamed and ran back into his house. Other voices, panicked, sounded from the homes now.

I waited no longer. I pulled Pippa into the shadows of the houses and ran for the trees that hedged the village. Here the mud disappeared and grass had taken root all the way to the woods. We were not alone. Pouring out from the backs of the houses, men, women, and children suddenly appeared, rushing to the forest. Some clutched bundles while others struggled to dress as they hurried through the morning grass. For a town that had seemed so unprepared, I was shocked at how quickly they made their escape. From the corner of my eye I caught sight of a figure on horseback charging from between two houses. People screamed and scattered.

"This way, Pippa!" We ran along the backs of the homes toward the end of the village. I had intended for us to leap straight into the trees once we were past the raiders, but a stone fence, higher than the one we had jumped at the farm, kept me searching for an opening. The land rose sharply again and I remembered the building close to the sea, the one we had seen from the heights.

The peak of a building came into view as we crested the hill. The wall now reached above my head.

"Back!" I tugged at Pippa.

She stared at the buildings. "No. This is right."

A single dwelling, made largely of stone, stood alone from the others, only a hundred steps from the beach. There was no time to take anything else in, for a robed figure suddenly filled the entrance.

"Come in, children. Quickly now."

I stopped and threw an arm in front of Pippa.

"Corki, this is right!" she whispered. "Keep going. It is a place of peace . . . I know it!"

"No, run for the trees."

"If we go back we will face the horsemen!"

Someone smashed a wooden door to splinters behind us.

"Stay close, Pippa. Very close."

The man stepped back to let us in. All over the inside walls, pictures stood out boldly and rows of benches filled the large room. I had never seen anything like it. It seemed a peaceful place.

The man hardly looked at us. When he turned to beckon us farther in, I glimpsed a bearded, deeply lined face. He was dressed in a brown robe that reached to his ankles. At the center of an adjoining room he stopped, and with a quick motion kicked a large fur aside. A wooden door with a ring of worn metal was cut into the floor. He gripped the ring, grunted, and raised the door. A stairway appeared, leading down into darkness. There was a strong odor, strange but not unpleasant, wafting up from the blackness.

"Quickly, children. Time is short."

I held Pippa back. "We do not know him. What if—"

"What else shall we do, Coriko?"

Hoofbeats sounded outside. I stepped around her and took the first steps down into the dark, Pippa close behind me. As the door swung closed I saw the man's furrowed face one last time.

The darkness was so deep I could not see the floor or Pippa.

She wrapped her arms around my waist. "It is cold."

"There are a few more steps. Let go of my waist," I whispered. "Where is your hand?"

I pointed my dagger ahead and poked the blackness. There was nothing directly in front of us. Instinctively I looked up. No light came in from the trapdoor. Someone yelled. It did not sound like the old man.

"Cellar." Pippa's lips brushed my ear.

We could not even use hand signals in the blackness. "What is *that*?" I asked her.

"A place to keep food and wine."

"Certain?"

"Yes. The smell. I remember."

We stood for many breaths, listening.

"Don't move." I stepped away, slowly, with my arms out, until I found each of the four walls. Pippa gripped me tightly when I came back.

"There is nothing here," I muttered. "Just a cold chamber."

There was a crash against the wooden door above us. I whirled Pippa around and pushed her to the floor. The knife shifted easily in my hand, poised for a throw. I reached the first step.

"We have to help him!" Pippa squealed.

"Quiet."

"Corki, we must help him."

"Why?"

Her voice crumbled. "Because I . . . because we *must*."

I made it to the third step. If they opened the door I would throw and hope they dropped a weapon down the stairs. For all the time I had trained as a Spear, I had learned to leap out of dark places, to use secrecy, night, and surprise to my advantage. If only Thief were at my back.

I held still. How smart were these raiders? A seasoned

warrior would fire an arrow down the steps before exposing himself to danger. Even if I escaped being hit there was a chance Pippa might be struck. I cursed myself for not going back to the trees when we had the chance.

"Get as far back as you can," I whispered. The voices above stopped. Something scraped across the wood. Keeping one hand on the stair for balance, I crouched and brought the dagger behind my head. A trickle of sweat burned my eye. I closed it tight then reopened it, as we had been trained. A soft knock above made me crouch even lower. The door opened a crack, enough to flood the stairs with light, but not enough for my knife to get through.

"Children?" The man's voice was unmistakable.

"We are here!" Pippa called from behind me.

I cringed.

She seemed desperate to get to the top of the stairs. I pushed her back to the floor. Could she never understand the danger? The door opened farther and the bearded face reappeared. I let my eyes adjust.

"They have gone," he said quietly. "And you may lower your dagger, little warrior. I daresay you know how to use it. I will not harm a hair of your head."

"Where are the soldiers?" I whispered. I did not lower my knife.

"They have taken some grain, a few coins." His brow crinkled. "And thirty bottles of my best wine from another cellar. A small price for two lives, although you are not the first to hide here. The soldiers have nearly reached the crest of the hill. A moment longer and I believe it will be safe. They show no intention of remaining."

I lowered my arm. Pippa tried to pass me.

I stopped her. "Let me go first."

"Allow me to check the road," our protector said as he disappeared. The floor creaked above us as he moved to the door. He returned shortly. "There is no danger at the moment," he said, "although it would be wise to remain indoors for a time. They have reached the gate. It was food they wanted this time."

He offered a hand. I ignored him and reached back to pull Pippa up. At the top step, I ran quickly to the door to peer out. Villagers poked their heads out from the near woods and a few walked back to their homes. Far beyond the gate I could see the dust cloud from the horses as the soldiers made their way back up the slope of the mountain. A chicken lay trampled in the mud: a strange shock of white in the churned black earth.

When I turned, Pippa covered her mouth. The man stared at her with equal interest. He carried some weight around his waist without being fat, and his hands rested comfortably at his hips. It was difficult to know his age. He was not anywhere near Mira's ninety-two summers, yet surpassed any Spear warrior I had known. He was, I decided, between them. His white-flecked hair was cropped close to his head, and his beard had long turned to gray. But what caught my attention more than anything was his eyes. They were green.

"Where are you from, child?" he said calmly.

Pippa did not speak. Her face was white. I walked over and stood in front of her. She clasped her hands around my stomach. Her chin rested on my shoulder.

"We are from across the sea." I waved in the direction of the water. His eyebrows went up.

"Across the sea? That is a long way."

"Why did you help us?" I asked. The door was close enough to reach if we had to, and I did not question that I could kill him. Still, the more he spoke the more I wondered about his skills. His confidence was total.

"Why would I not? Raiders do not make exceptions for those whom they pillage and God makes no exception for those He will save. Why should I do any less? I protect any who are sent to me."

His tone was not unkind. *Why did his eyes never leave Pippa?*

I snorted. "We were not *sent* to you. I would have hidden in the forest and saved us the fear of being trapped in a hole."

For the first time since I had come up the stairs he looked straight at me. "Lad, I have lived long enough to know that the best gifts are given without our asking, and the little roads we take when lost are often the ones that lead us home."

I nodded toward the mountains. "Who are these raiders?"

He grunted. "An evil brood. A ceaseless host that continues to grow and search for more. Long ago they came from the east, built their fortresses, and took over this land. Their dominion increases each year and swallows town after town. Our little village has survived only because of our farms. They need the food we grow, and seldom attack too quickly after a raid, so that our crops can grow again. The people have learned to escape at a moment's notice, as you have seen. There is little else they can do, except clean up the mess and start again."

"Why do they not flee far away?" I asked.

"A man would have to travel across the sea to get away from raiders, I think. It is not easy to take a family far enough away on foot. Some have left. Some have returned when nothing better was found. Many men and women have been lost trying to resist. My heart tells me that this cannot continue. Sometime soon the raiders will take everything we have. Our farms will become their farms and in our homes, strangers will wake and sleep. There is little law in the land." He shook his head. "I am surprised you have not seen them. Even if you come from across the sea."

"We have seen them," Pippa said. "They are the Outside army."

His smile faded. "Your voice . . . your face . . ."

Although he was not a tall man, who could not have

stood up to Marumuk, his arms were as thick as a farmer's, and from experience I knew their danger.

"Stay back, old one. You saved us from the raiders and for that I do not wish to harm you. But you must not come near Pippa."

He blanched at her name and to my complete surprise dropped to one knee as if I had struck him.

"Pippa," he croaked.

I crouched, ready to spring. Pippa dug her fingers into my shoulder. "Get behind me, Pippa. Now."

She did not move.

"Pippa," the man said again, his hands clasped in prayer, his eyes closed tight.

"Let go of me, Corki."

"We do not know him!"

"I know him." Her voice trembled. "I know him."

2

IT WAS DIFFICULT TO WATCH SUCH powerful arms wrapped around Pippa without rushing to help her. Yet she did not struggle or call out. Instead, she collapsed in the man's embrace. Both of them wept. I moved behind him so I could read Pippa's face. She looked at me through happy tears. How small she seemed. Smiling, she reached out to me, and I took her hand. The man released her, allowing me to draw close.

"Who is this young warrior who watches over my daughter so carefully?"

Daughter.

She pulled me fiercely to her side, kissed my cheek, then laughed at my confusion. "This is Coriko. My heart, my love, my protector." She hugged me again.

The man raised his eyebrows.

To me she said, "And this is my father."

I stared from one pair of green eyes to the other.

"Coriko." He tasted my name thoughtfully. Beneath his steady gaze I could see the wisdom of an elder, the strength of a warrior, and a faith that matched his daughter's. He measured me up and down and pursed his lips. "My thanks," he said. "More than you will ever know . . . my thanks. And welcome to this house of prayer."

Then he turned and, laughing, kissed the top of Pippa's head. The smell of herbs, plants, and earth was all about his robe.

"Corki," Pippa mumbled happily.

When the tears slowed her father stood up. "My questions are so many I can hardly breathe."

"As are mine." Pippa did not let go of either of us. Her gaze swept the dwelling. "Where is my mother? And my sister?"

Her father traced a finger around her face. "You are so much like them. Come with me. Words will not do just yet."

We followed his sweeping robes to the back of the

dwelling, past the painted walls, and through a large wooden door. The sea, less than a hundred strides away, crashed below the gray sky. Before us a neatly kept pasture covered most of the distance to the beach. But there was no grain here. Scattered throughout the field were small marking stones lying in the short grass. It looked much like the graveyard we had found near the Spear village nearly four seasons ago. Only this one was in much better condition. Someone had carefully painted the stones and kept the grasses low.

On either side of the graveyard lay spreading gardens. My eye was not trained for such things, but it was not difficult to see the fruit trees, vines, and turned soil reaching all the way to the trees and sea.

"It is beautiful, Father," Pippa whispered.

He took her hand. "Yes. And with the spring, brightly colored flowers will grow in abundance. This is my place of peace."

I looked up in surprise at the familiar saying.

He sighed. "When I am not tending to the needs of the people, this is where I rest."

"Where is my mother?" Pippa asked again.

"Your mother is here."

Pippa said nothing as he led us out among the stones.

He stopped as we drew close to the sea, and turned to face a small group of stones, one large and two small. Words had been cut into each.

Pippa gasped and dropped to her knees, her small hands touching the letters. Although we had not practiced our writing since Grassland, I recognized the symbols on the largest stone. Pippa had made the markings many times on the floor of our cell.

Mother.

More was written on the same stone, but I could not read it.

"She did not live past the night you were taken from us," her father said quietly. "Her wounds were great. If comfort can be found, it is that she did not wake to find you gone." He knelt beside his daughter and touched one of the smaller stones gently. "Of this one I cannot speak. It was my hope that you would know the answer."

Pippa swept a speck of dirt from the letters. "I do not know if Kisha lived. But I took care of her until the Spears made me leave her behind. I called 'peace' to her until she

27

was too far away to hear." She sat up and breathed deeply. "There is hope."

The old man lifted his daughter's chin. "Even that a daughter may return from the dead."

I stared at the vast fields. I thought of the ones we had run through on our way down the hillside to warn the village. In the fall, this place would yield an enormous crop.

The old man wrestled with one of the smaller stones. "This no longer belongs here." With a mighty heave he pushed it back, churning up the earth around it. Then he pulled it toward him, tearing it from the ground.

He began to stagger, with the stone wrapped in his burly arms, toward the sea. I followed, curious. He stepped onto the beach and into the water, the hem of his robe soaked instantly by the waves. Gathering up his strength, he bent his knees and hurled the stone into the air. It landed with an enormous splash. When he regained his balance he raised a fist. "Gone! For my Pippa has returned."

Then he swung away from the sea, and gathering Pippa again in his arms, kissed her on both cheeks. "Do you know that last night was the first time in nine summers that I have not dreamed of doing that? My heart has often said that Pippa's stone should not be resting in the field."

Shaking my head, I followed father and daughter back to the house. If Pippa was hard to understand at times, this man was even more confusing.

The house, I learned, was not like the other village dwellings. It was a structure made by all the people, and for all the people. Pippa called it a church. It was a place where they came to pray, to discuss, to bury, and to hope. Her father lived there.

"On the night your mother died and I lost you and Kisha," he explained as he poured a clear liquid into mugs, "I found myself here, at this church. I was covered in wounds and lay on the floor hoping desperately for my last breath." He pushed a mug at me. "When I did not die I awoke to discover that my hurts had been bound and that I lay on a soft bed with wine and food beside me." He glanced at his daughter. "It was old Lieflund who saved me."

"Father Lieflund!" Pippa repeated.

"Yes, the same. The old man would not let me die. I did not speak a word to him or any other man for a year.

As my strength returned, he took me each day out to the garden to tend the fruits and till the soil. We harvested the grain, baked bread, made wine, buried the dead, took care of the sick, and even settled disputes between neighbors. The cellar you hid in"—he gestured with his head—"was the last of five that we dug with our own hands. Lieflund believed they would be needed as the raiders . . . What did you call them?"

"Outside. They are the Outside army," I said.

"Well, Lieflund believed these Outsiders would come more often. And they have!"

He sighed again. "I learned more about plants and herbs than I thought possible. Writing is not common among the people, so Lieflund was delighted when he discovered I had the skill. My nights were soon spent poring over his journals, discovering all his knowledge about the proper tending of a garden. It was when the candles burned low and the books were put away that my burdens returned. My dreams plagued me. Lieflund would pray each night, kneeling at my bedside until the evil left."

Pippa's father folded his hands as if in prayer. "Every day he told me that I had been spared for a purpose. He

30

said that this had always been my first place, my first calling. At the beginning I could only smile bitterly at his words. But as the people continued to come here for help, I found myself slowly caring about the faces that knelt and prayed at the benches. My heart grieved with those who came to bury loved ones, and hardly were my hands clean of the dirt from a grave when I was being called to pray over a newborn. Their daily troubles worked their way into my life so much, there was less time for my own grief."

Pippa watched her father with unblinking eyes.

"When Father Lieflund died three winters ago, it did not enter my mind to leave. Nor did the people expect it. I had to receive the blessing from Father Bergoin in Gotten, but once that was done, the people continued to come as they always had. The garden needed tending, and with the last few winters being more harsh than usual, I seemed to be handing out more healing herbs than ever."

I took a sip of the drink and screwed my eyes up tight. It was difficult to get down, and burned as it went.

"That's good ale, lad," he said, laughing. "You won't find better in any village in these parts."

Despite his encouragement I decided that water would be best, and asked for some.

He left the room. While he was out I whispered to Pippa, "We must find the others. They will be wondering where we are."

"Yes. I will tell my father."

He saw us whispering as he entered, and grinned. "Ah, me. Now, Daughter, *your* story remains untold. I am hungry to hear everything that has happened to you."

"Father," Pippa began, "there are more of us, hiding in the woods, in the hills. We need to let them know we are safe."

He nodded. "Of course. They may come here. How many?"

"Eight more," I answered.

"Are any of these older than you?"

"No."

Shaking his head, he rose from the table. "All this way, without the aid of a single gray head? Come. Let us go and collect your friends. They will be as hungry as you, I imagine."

"Is there a danger from the villagers?"

"No, no." He waved my worries away. "Not with me at your side. I have saved enough lives in this little town to earn the respect of every family for generations to come. I go as I please and do as I like. Your tiny band will raise eyebrows and questions, nothing more."

The woods beyond the farm were unsettlingly quiet. Even with Pippa's father beside us I could not help wanting to stay closer to the trees rather than walk on the road, but he walked with a purpose, his staff in his hand and lines of worry creasing his brow.

"At least there was no burning," he mumbled.

"Do they attack often?" Pippa walked quickly to keep up.

"Their raids are disorganized and haphazard at best. Their self-proclaimed king, Rokhan, gives more and more power to his relatives, who in turn raid us without conferring with one another. So we sleep with our bags packed. How much more they think they can steal from us, God only knows."

We came to the first farm we had crossed in our run from the forest. The farmer and his family watched us approach.

"Hello, Lars," the churchman called. "Any trouble here?"

"No, Father," came the reply. He stared at us curiously. "They rode on through. How did the village fare?"

"Food and wine, my friend. Mostly mine too, confound them! Nothing more. No damage that I have heard so far. God protect us."

"God protect us, Father. Keep praying!"

"Always, Lars. Always."

Thief was the first to reveal himself. He watched the old man warily but, encouraged by my smile, stepped out from the trees.

"Where have you been?" he whispered. "And who is this?"

"This is Pippa's father."

Thief's eyes showed surprise, but when he looked to Pippa to confirm what I had said, and saw her smile, he grunted with satisfaction.

"He is important in this village," I continued, "and can give us food and shelter. Bring the others out. The raiders have left."

Thief nodded. "I saw them go. But Feelah would not let me follow them."

"She is wiser than you, my friend."

He grinned and headed back into the woods.

"I have never seen anyone with dark skin," the churchman said quietly. "I have heard about them. Father Lieflund had been to their country before and spoke about it often. You have learned their speech."

"We speak a common tongue," Pippa answered. "It is not the language of our friends. It is the language of our captors, the Spears who took me from here."

He nodded. "Of course. Then these have all escaped the . . . Spears . . . with you?"

"Yes."

He rubbed his chin. "Wonder upon wonders."

Feelah led the group out and soon they huddled around, staring at the man among us.

"From far and wide," Father mumbled. He stooped to ruffle the hair of the nearest child. "You are welcome here, children. All of you. There is food and water, and a place to sleep."

Pippa smiled. "Most of them cannot understand you, Father."

"Yah. I understand," Feelah said. She pointed to Father. "This man is Pippa's father. He will give us food."

Living in a cramped boat for almost four seasons had forced the children to learn the Spear language quickly. One of them squealed with excitement at the word *food*.

With a nod Father turned and walked toward the road. It was comforting to see one of the children reach for his hand before they had gone ten strides. Bran, I noticed, walked at the front, speaking freely, as if he had known the man all his life.

Feelah nudged me. "What do they call him?"

"Father."

"All of them?"

"Yes."

She shrugged. "He must have many wives."

Pippa scowled. "He does not have many wives. He is *my* father."

Feelah looked at me. "Whose father is he?"

"Pippa's."

She looked at Thief in confusion.

I sighed. "The people of the village call him *Father* because he is someone who takes care of everyone. He is a healer. He prays for them. Like Pippa."

"Ahhhhh," they said together.

Walking through the village again was completely different from our first experience. Everywhere we looked people were gathered in small groups, clustered at doors, or standing on the road. They watched our approach with expressions of friendly curiosity.

I was equally interested. This was the first time I had been able to look openly at a group of people from the North in the daylight. The villagers stopped talking the moment we entered the gate. Their clothes were not colorful, and looked more practical than what we had seen in the Spear village in Grassland. These were more like the old work-cloths we had worn when the Spears ruled us—made for working, for warmth against the chill, and to keep the sun away by day as we worked in Grassland's fields. It was strange to see men and women together. Some comforted others. There were many soldiers in Grassland, but we seldom saw them with their mates.

The people's gaze washed over me to fall on Thief

and Feelah. My friends returned the stares. Feelah pressed closer to Father, and Thief, I noticed, kept his hand near the sword at his side.

"Why do they stare at me so much?" he whispered.

"Your skin is as dark as buried earth," I answered. "Look at them, Thief! They are pale in this place. You are strange to their eyes."

He grunted.

"I do not like the staring," Feelah whispered over Thief's shoulder.

"Father said no harm will come to us," I assured her. "And do not worry, Feelah. Thief and I are good with our swords. Let them stare. And let them be certain that is all they do."

Pippa's father herded our group toward the church, keeping each one within arm's reach.

"How do you fare, Father?" a man finally asked.

"All is well," he replied. "Today's raid was to my gain, for my daughter is brought back to me!"

The man's eyes never left Thief. "We lost two chickens and a dog. The Gaardsons lost two barrels of last fall's apples. Knarlf is just checking the straw—we think they may have taken the last of the salt pork. It should have been hidden in the cellars, but there was no time last night."

"They took yesterday's bread, father!" a woman called out.

"Ease your hearts, friends," Pippa's father answered. "It could have been worse. We still have our children. Look at these! They have lost their parents. Tell the Gaardsons I have enough apples for them as well. Tell everyone to come up the hill tonight. There will be food for all! Let the raiders know that our spirits are not dampened!"

"Who are the children, Father?" someone asked.

"I do not yet know." He smiled. "We will find out soon enough. And they will be well taken care of. But there will be a celebration tonight, for my daughter has come home!"

3

THE VILLAGERS' TORCHES SHONE
brightly as they topped the hill at nightfall. Standing at the
door of the church, Thief and I watched their approach
with interest.

"Strange, this place," he said quietly. "They are
attacked, their food is stolen, and then they celebrate."

I snorted. "They do not celebrate because they were
attacked, idiot. Father celebrates because his daughter
has come home. The church has the most supplies, so
he shares it with the village."

Pippa worked beside her father in the inner room,
preparing the food we had carried up from the cellars.
The church held more secrets than I could have
imagined. A larger chamber, deeper than the one where

we had hidden, was built into the floor. The entrance for this lay behind the wall with all the paintings. Just as we hid things from the Spears when we lived in our cells in Grassland, these villagers hid their treasures from those who would take them. I thought about all the settlements we had traveled to before finally reaching Pippa's village. Perhaps there were *no* safe places. Not anywhere.

In the cellar below the painted wall were barrels of ale and wine, roots of various kinds needing to be cropped and washed, and crushed grain for making hearth bread. Pippa was eager to help with all of it, carrying, cutting, cooking. Every time I tried to speak with her, Father called for her to help. There was no time to speak or plan. Although she smiled at me often, I could not stop a feeling of change creeping into my heart.

Father stopped frequently to touch her hair, kiss her forehead, or smile. But I could not let myself be angry with him. His love flowed easily toward all of us, and a scowl did not last long in his presence. He had also taken over the needs of the children we had brought with us as if they were his own.

"We'll find a place for each of them!" he assured Pippa. "If nowhere else, then here."

Frieda, the young girl I had stolen on my first raid as a Red Fist, now grinned back at me. She followed Pippa like a duckling after its mother. We had not found her village in our travels, and while I could not hope that she would ever find her home again, my heart was the better for seeing her safe with Father.

Thief regarded the flickering torches being carried up the hill. He nudged my shoulder. "So much food. But so soon after a raid?"

The torchlight glowed eerily and the smell of burning oil wafted up the hill. My breath billowed in small clouds. "I would hide more food in the cellars, set up a watch, gather all the weapons we had, and hide in the woods," I said.

He grunted. "That is what we should be doing. I am feeling helpless without my sword. I do not think the Father was right to make us keep them in the cellar."

Bran came up behind us carrying a mug. His hair was braided and he was wearing a different tunic. Like Pippa, he seemed at home in this place, frequently talking to

Father and using the tools of the village with ease. He held out the mug. "You should try this," he said. "It's good."

"No."

He shrugged and handed it to Thief. My friend took a sniff. He crinkled his nose and sipped. With a smile, he drained the ale in one long gulp.

"Pippa says not to drink very much of that," I warned him.

His eyes were shining. "Are we celebrating or hiding, Coriko?"

I snorted.

Bran grinned and raised his mug. "One more drink of this and he won't be doing either. He'll be sleeping."

"No more, Bran," I growled. "We need him awake tonight. All of us."

He raised the glass in surprise. "Why?"

I moved away from the door as the first of the villagers approached. "I do not know." He stared at me for a long while, then set the mug on a near table. "I'll keep my eyes open."

Eight families made up the village, some of them with as many as seven children. It was no wonder that Father was kept busy giving herbs for sickness. For a long while there was talk and scattered stories of the day's events. While the children's parents talked, little ones tumbled about on the floor. Their noses streamed and there was hardly a moment when one of them was not having a coughing fit. It did not seem to slow them down.

The food lay steaming on a table at one end of the room. The villagers helped themselves to hot apples, vegetables, ale, and some of Father's salted meat. Each family had brought their own plates and mugs, which made me think that Father had done this sort of thing before. The warmth from the hearth soothed my muscles.

I watched Pippa move from one group to another, pouring ale and receiving welcome. Mothers, fathers, young men and women, children, all flowed about the room, living as if no raiders had come this day. Pippa's father rarely left her side, and both laughed so often I wondered if she had forgotten about me. Feelah and Thief sat with me in a corner, our backs to the open door. Bran was somewhere close by, but I had not seen him for a while.

"Look at her, Coriko." Feelah interrupted my thoughts. "She is so happy. And look at her dress!"

I noticed. I could not help but notice. Her father had given her a dress that afternoon. It was not as colorful as the Spear clothes she had worn, but it fit her perfectly.

"It was her mother's," Feelah finished.

"I know," I answered gloomily.

"She looks good," Thief spoke up. "Pretty."

"This is where she belongs," Feelah whispered to me. "You must be so happy."

I stood. "I need some air."

I stepped out into the night. The half moon shone across the sea, lighting my way. *Too bright. Too bright. We needed clouds to hide us. Where was Bran?*

I walked behind the church, past the laughing voices and dancing candlelight, past the graveyard and toward the sound of the pounding surf. The air was cooler here and the salt breeze drowned out all the noise from the church. I sat for a while, my back against a tall piece of driftwood, letting the wind bathe my face and wondering why I had let my thoughts disturb me. It was not long before I felt, rather than heard, someone behind me. I whirled, cursing myself for leaving my sword in the cellar.

"Why are you here?" Pippa crossed her arms over her

45

new dress, her unbraided hair whipping about her head. Her face was flushed from the warmth of the church, and the completeness of her beauty startled me. Thief was right. Pippa was pretty. Beautiful.

"Coriko. Why are you not inside? Why are you not celebrating?"

"I don't feel right in there," I stammered. "I came to watch the waves." When she did not speak I added, "I do not even know *how* to celebrate. These are not my people. They are your people. We came all this way to get here, all this way, through danger and ocean. And now . . . it seems as if you have found what you were looking for, but I have not. When we met your father, I was hoping that our journey had ended. It does not feel ended to me now."

She took my face in both her hands. The moon had found her eyes, so bright, so shining. "*You* are my home."

I kissed her.

Her hands eased from my face and wrapped around my neck, pulling me to her. We had kissed before, but not like this. This was something that had never happened in Grassland. My arms were around her and I told her my heart, my fears, and my hopes through that one long kiss.

When I pulled away, her eyes danced and she hugged me tightly, offering her face so that I could kiss her again.

Before our lips touched, something struck me hard in the side. The air wheezed out of my chest and we landed on the beach, still locked in our embrace, with someone on top of us.

"Coriko!" a voice hissed.

"What is—?"

"Be silent!"

It was Bran. His hair was covered in bracken and his face was as white as a sea bird in the moonlight.

"Follow!" he whispered.

"What is it?"

"More raiders have come."

We scrambled up.

"Frieda and the other children," Pippa gasped. "We have brought them from danger into more danger!"

I pulled her back. "Wait. Let me think. Let me plan." I turned to Bran. "Where are they? How many?"

He struggled to get his breath back. "Can't tell. They are

47

on horseback. At least, some of them are. I stayed out near the woods because you said you were uneasy. Sure enough, they came only moments ago. Father has barricaded the doors. No one could get out in time. I saw you and Pippa leave and come this way, so I raced here." He paused to breathe. "It is bad, Coriko. They have surrounded the church. And I do not like what they intend."

"What?" Pippa leaned forward, all color draining from her face.

He looked at me. "I do not think these soldiers are here just for food or drink. They are here to make trouble—for the sport of it." His frown deepened. "I think they mean to burn the church. With everyone in it."

Pippa was up before I could grab her. She lifted her skirt and ran.

I leaped up and caught her before she reached the grasses. She struggled briefly, then burst into a sob.

"My way, Pippa!" I whispered. "We do this my way this time."

She nodded, still sobbing. Bran joined us and together we looked out from behind the roots of a driftwood log.

The moonlight revealed a terrible scene. Soldiers

surrounded the church. Their horses were tied up well back from the building, two of them only fifty strides from where we lay hidden. Three raiders with burning brands in their fists stood at the back door. A few others waited at the side of the building, and still another was making his way to the front.

"Looks like a vanguard," I whispered.

"A what?"

"Vanguard. The end of a band of soldiers. These are likely part of the group that struck this morning, but were held up for some reason and did not come with the others. They must have decided to do their own raiding as well."

"At least they can't burn a stone church," Bran said.

Pippa hissed, "The roof is wood and thatch. It will burn."

I counted the soldiers again. "I can take two of them. There are weapons on the horses. I can see them from here."

"I don't think I could even take one," Bran squeaked. "I don't have your training."

"If only we could get Thief out," I murmured. "Can you shoot an arrow?"

Bran pulled a face. "You do all the hunting."

I slapped the ground. "We *have* to get Thief out."

Pippa's face streamed tears, but she spoke steadily enough. "If you distract them at the front of the church, it might draw the others from the back. Bran and I could open the door. We would have to pray that Thief would be there." She paused. "It's a terrible risk. The soldiers will return quickly when they hear people running out through the graveyard. But some villagers might get away."

I smiled grimly. "You would make a good soldier, Pippa. I think that might work."

One of the raiders held his burning brand in the air. He began yelling something to those in the church in a harsh, evil-sounding language. I turned to Bran. "If it doesn't work, run for the woods. Stay there until morning. I will meet you both back here at daylight. It does not look as if they mean to give us much time."

Heedless of Bran, I kissed Pippa before breaking cover.

"Find me!" she whispered fiercely.

"Always."

"No killing, please."

50

I did not answer.

The raider continued to yell at the church. The sound of his words was taunting, as if he was daring the people to come out. Soon the other raiders joined him until their shouts became a chant. Keeping low to the ground, I stole my way to the horses. With the crashing surf at my back I did not fear being overheard until I was close. And I did not mean to get too close until I had to. It was the horses I was concerned about. If they started, it might raise the alarm.

I was no more than ten strides away when they noticed me. The first horse turned its head and stamped. Another flared its nostrils. None of them whinnied, so I continued until I was right among them. Stroking their sweat-soaked sides, I spoke soothingly, feeling for their saddles. There were bows and quivers tied behind the saddles. Five neatly clipped arrows gleamed back at me.

I had only a little training with bow and arrow under Marumuk, but three seasons of hunting for game had made me a good shot.

Before slipping away, I eased the horses' tethers loose. The horses provided good cover as I made my way around the garden. Only three raiders there—seven in total. They

51

did not fear or respect the village defenses to attack with only seven. How easily Pippa and her sister must have been taken by Spears the first time. The thought of my Pippa being ripped from her home gave me new urgency.

I knelt with my back against a fruit tree. The bow was well-made and the arrow slipped perfectly onto the string. The beach was deserted and there was no sign of Pippa or Bran. The moon gave me all the light I needed. Keeping my arm firm and my shoulders relaxed, I drew the arrow back.

Breathe . . . slow . . . strength . . . Marumuk's words sounded in my head, quiet and confident. The lead raider laughed and turned to face the others. He held his torch high and made to throw it onto the roof. I aimed for his chest and let the arrow fly. He spun sideways as the arrow took him high, near the throat, then fell to the ground with the torch still blazing in his hand.

"Sorry, Pippa," I muttered.

The soldiers stopped shouting. Two drew their swords. One made for the horses. He fell soundlessly with my second arrow.

"Sorry, Pippa," I muttered again and reached for another. The third arrow I aimed at the horses. Picking a spot near the ground, I sent it skittering among their feet. One of them reared and, breaking their tethers, they fled at a panicked gallop into the woods. The remaining soldiers fled from the graveyard, one of them chasing the horses and the others running toward their fallen companions.

It would not be long before I was discovered, yet I took the time to patiently find one more target.

"Yah, Coriko!"

Thief's voice startled me. My arrow flew wildly over the soldiers' heads and imbedded in the church door.

"Idiot!" I hissed.

"Sword." He tossed it hilt first. "Bran and Pippa have most of the people in the woods. There are still some in the church."

"We need more arrows," I said. "Two soldiers are down, another has gone after the horses. Four remain."

Thief shook his head. "Not any more." He lifted his knife. "I met one on my way here." His arm was bleeding above the elbow.

Pippa was not going to be happy. "Let's take the other three and pray that no more are coming."

Together we strode out into the moonlight. The

remaining soldiers were terrified, turning at every sound, ready to scatter. They kept low, waiting for more arrows to come, yet too fearful to enter the woods. At the sight of us they froze, staring in disbelief at our raised swords.

Suddenly the church door burst open and Father appeared, waving his large staff. At his side several young farmers wielded chunks of firewood. The soldiers ran for the road and reached the crest of the hill before we were within fighting distance.

One lone figure turned back. He picked up a handful of dirt and threw it in our direction. He shouted and slashed the air. I had seen such taunts before. He was threatening to come back and destroy everything.

"Come back *now*, little man," Thief yelled as the soldier disappeared after the others.

Father watched him with knitted brows.

Feelah grabbed her Thief.

"You were supposed to go with the others," he scolded.

She laughed, staring after the soldiers. "Look at Father! I was behind him, so I knew I was safe."

Father came over to us. "How do you fare, my son?"

"All is well. For now. Who was that last soldier? The one who taunted us?"

Father glanced at the fallen men only strides away. His eyes lingered on the feathers of the arrows thrusting up in the moonlight.

I wiped my sweaty hair from my face. "I am sorry," I said. He was so much like Pippa, the words came from my mouth as if she had been standing there herself. "I had little choice."

His hand went to my shoulder. "You continue to astonish me, lad. I long to hear your history and can only pray that we are given the time to enjoy it. Thank you for risking your life to save others."

As more villagers approached, he whispered, "The raider you spoke of is the king's cousin—a wretched vagabond who has been here too often for our liking. He has a taste for our ale. The people will be doubly afraid now that you have earned his anger."

"Father!" Pippa's voice rang out above the clamoring people. She launched herself at both of us.

"Pippa!" Feelah intercepted her. She glanced at me,

then briefly at the dead man behind us. "Come back to the church. My Thief has gone and cut himself. He needs your healing." She took Pippa by the shoulders and led her, with Thief following, blocking the grisly sight. I blew out a long breath.

Bran clapped my shoulder.

"Well done, friend," I said. "You alone kept watch."

His smile was as full as it could get without breaking into laughter.

The people clustered around Father. Not all of them were looking at me with enthusiasm.

"What will we do, Father?" the one named Garth said. "The king's cousin will come back. And with the army. We are in more danger than ever before. Blood should not have been shed. Better we let them take what they wanted, as we have always done."

Father quieted the crowd. "And what would you have done, Garth? It was only a matter of time before they lit the church on fire. King's cousin or not, what would we have done? Would you have killed to save your children? What choice was left?"

The man did not answer. He watched me uneasily.

No one seemed eager to go back into the church despite the cold, and many watched the road with furtive looks.

"Garth is right on one account," Father said. "We must do something."

"Yes," I murmured. The tiny cloud of dust at the top of the hill had hardly settled from their retreat, and yet I knew it would not be the last we saw of the raiders. Marumuk would not have suffered such a disgrace. Retribution was swift in Grassland, and without mercy. I did not doubt it would be any different here. "Is there a safe place for the villagers to hide? Are there caves we could go to, a refuge of some kind?"

Father and Garth shook their heads. "It is an unforgiving hand that rules us," the older man said. "You called them 'Outside,' Coriko. We know them as Rokhan's army. We have been warned before that if we should so much as raise a pitchfork against the raiders, Rokhan will burn all we have to the ground."

An older woman began to weep.

"Peace, Edwina!" Father said. "Trouble is not new to us. Good faith, all! Let us think and pray."

Garth gripped my arm. "The soldiers *will* return. The king's cousin will have his revenge and they will come for all of us. They will search the woods, the coast, everywhere."

Facing the church, Father put his hands on his hips. He sighed deeply. All eyes turned to him. His gaze swept the orchards and fields and, finally, the people. "Father Lieflund once reminded me: 'Do not set your heart on stone, or field or trees. These will all fail in time. For stones crumble, fields change with the seasons, and trees become fuel for fires. Rather, follow the way of faith, hope, and love, for these will not wither for a thousand ages.'"

There was a murmur of assent at the name *Lieflund*.

"Yet in a moment, in a twinkling, our lives are changed. Through sweat and toil we raised this place," Father continued. "And we can toil again in another. Friends, I am afraid the time has come for us to leave." An unhappy silence followed.

"Where will we go, then?" Garth spoke again.

Father scratched his chin. "To Gotten. There is nowhere else with enough fortifications. And I am known to the church there. I have great hope that the brothers will pay a recompense for us."

"A recompense?" I asked.

"There are times when soldiers are willing to take money instead of blood for revenge. Gotten is a large town, and Father Bergoin is a generous man. I believe he would put forward many coins on our behalf. It may be enough to satisfy Rokhan."

"How far to Gotten?" I asked.

"Two days," he answered. "Maybe more with so many children."

"Where are the nearest Outsiders posted?"

Father looked at Garth.

"At Berge—half a day by horse, no more," Garth said. "But the king's cousin has to get there first and tell his story," he continued. "He is walking, thanks to Coriko and Thief. It is a two-day journey to Berge, even if they ran some of the way. At best, we have five days. And we must hope that no other soldiers stop as these did."

"Father," I said quietly. "The dead must be removed and hidden, the horses found and kept out of sight. If

59

any other soldiers come here before a day is out they cannot see anything that will raise suspicion."

He nodded. "Good lad."

"A watch should be set," Bran added.

"Aye. And provisions." Father sighed. "Father Lieflund would be proud that all our hard work in building those cellars and storing provisions is about to save the town." He squared his shoulders. "Ah, me. Just when the celebration begins, another task is given."

We made for the church, leaving them to begin the long labor. I was grateful they did not ask for help with the burials. Bran kept close to my side as we approached the others. Thief was seated on a bench, his eyes scrunched in pain. He sipped from a mug of ale. Feelah held a steaming cloth to his arm while Pippa stitched the wound.

I sat down beside him. "Why do you always injure *that* arm?"

"Shut up, Coriko," he muttered through gritted teeth.

"I hear that a lot from you."

Pippa was strangely quiet, and I wondered if she had been told of my night's work. Feelah took my hand and squeezed it. "When do we leave?"

4

I T TOOK THREE DAYS TO REACH
Gotten. We left at night to avoid being seen. Several of
the children were sick, and to make matters worse, it
rained on the second day. We took a less traveled road
to avoid being seen, only to be bogged down in mud.
Four of the seven horses had been found and I trudged
beside one of them, gripping its long mane from time
to time when the mud grew thick and sucked at my
feet. Their saddles had been removed, buried in the
orchard, and replaced with blankets. Even with the
horses carrying supplies, there was hardly an empty
hand in the group. There was little hope of returning
to Pippa's village.

"We've been a long time in this place," Father said

the eve we left. "It's not easy to simply walk away from something that has shaped your life."

They were a strong people. Despite the hardships of being conquered, they had persevered, struggling to work their fields and gardens to produce enough to eat. They had learned ways to hide their goods from the Outside army. Some, like Father, had built cellars, while others slung their treasures between trees, hidden in the high canopy, to keep the raiders from taking everything. How similar the ways were to Grassland!

Pippa had not spoken to me since the night of the raid. When she found out about the dead soldiers, her face had gone red and she turned away. She walked with Father at the front of the line.

"Give her time," Bran told me. He did not seem bothered by the cold. Since coming to the North, he was as cheerful as ever, and even more so after meeting Father. He had recently fallen into the habit of whistling, which bothered me like flies around my face.

"Stop whistling, Bran," I muttered.

"Why?"

"You announce us to every ear within a thousand strides."

He stopped.

"Does this cold never end?" I grumbled, swinging my cloak closer around my neck.

"It is like this until later in the spring," he replied happily. "And this isn't really cold. At the height of winter you can throw water out the door and it will be frozen by the time you step out to look at it."

I stifled a moan.

He sniffed. "I thought you soldiers were supposed to handle hardships."

"I am not a soldier," I answered. "The Spears made me a Red Fist against my will. They took Pippa away from me. I did not choose the skills I have. My hands have blood on them, Bran. And I have learned enough to hope that I will not have to use these abilities anymore." What I did not say was that I sensed it would be only too soon before I was forced to act like a Spear again.

"Anyway," Bran continued. "About Pippa—she always comes back. To you, that is. And she always forgives."

He was right. But sometimes Pippa could be so stubborn.

"Think, Coriko. She even forgave the Spears!"

I nodded glumly and trudged on with my own thoughts. How quickly things could change! Only a few nights before, we had been excited at the hope of meeting Pippa's family. Now we traveled along a road of mud with an army coming after us.

"Bran is right," Feelah said, coming up to us. "Pippa is angry for a little while. Not long."

Thief kept looking behind us. He flexed his hands constantly and kept his cloak tied back to allow easy access to his sword. Our helmets, tied to the horse's sides, were within reach. He knew what I felt. It would only be a matter of time before scouts picked up our trail. Fleeing to Gotten was madness. We should have taken the boat and left this place, taking Father with us. But Pippa would have none of it.

"Coriko."

I looked up. Father had stopped the line and was waiting for me. Pippa stared blankly at the road ahead. "We are close to the town, now. Any moment we should reach the first farms. There will be some traffic on the road and I will have to explain why we are here. Messages will be sent ahead to Gotten." He frowned. "It troubles me that we have not seen anyone. There should have been carts bringing food for market." He eased the heavy sack from his shoulder. "I pray that there have been no raids here lately." Pippa stepped away, and I sighed.

"What are the town's defenses?"

"Much better than our little village. They have huge walls and a gate that is not easily breached. The town used to be a fort at one time, until the abbey took it over. They have a good-sized church and we will be given shelter there, I hope. But it is no promise of safety. If these raiders will burn a church, they'll burn a whole town."

"Then why did we come here?" I asked angrily.

He drew in a large breath. "Because of hope, my son. And because we had no other option than to come someplace where we might beg for safety. There is still hope that the raiders will turn aside, that they will seek no further revenge than what they do with the village. Or that they will accept what money Bergoin can offer. And do not discount divine intervention."

I shook my head. "It is a slim hope."

"Yet hope nonetheless."

"Yes."

He looked at me curiously. "Your coming to us seems to be a good example of it. I never expected to see my daughter again . . . yet I did." He hoisted his pack. "If I am wrong in my choice, if Gotten asks us to leave, or the army comes to this place"—his eyes drifted to his daughter—"I ask you to flee. Take her with you to a safe place. I know you will find one. It is your life, it is what you know how to do. Pippa has already told me this much."

"I do not think she would go anywhere with me right now," I said.

"We are often the most angry with the ones we love best. She loves you with all her heart, Coriko." He mopped his brow. "This was not the welcome I wished for my daughter," he murmured. "Or the reception I would give the man of her choice."

My face flushed. "I will take her to safety."

"Good! My heart is the better for it. Now, my son, do us all a good turn. Take her by the hand and sort out your differences before we reach the town. God's mercy,

I had forgotten what stubbornness was in my blood." He wiped away a smile. "I think I will drop back and join the horses." With a wink, he made his way down the line of weary travelers, shouting encouragement as he went.

I turned from him to find Pippa walking slowly in the direction of the town. When I caught up to her, all words left my head. "This place . . . this land is cold, Pippa," I stammered.

She tossed her head. "Not in our hearts." There was a long silence. "Why did you kill those men?" She would not look at me.

"Because they were going to kill the others. Thief, Feelah, Father . . . you."

"And you know this for certain? You saw inside their hearts?"

I took a deep breath. "No. But my eyes saw enough for me to believe, with all my heart, that terrible harm was going to come to my friends, and to you most of all. I will not let that happen while there is strength in my hands. You were there, Pippa. You saw the trouble with your own eyes."

Pippa nodded. "Yes. I did." She stopped walking and turned to me. From the corner of my eyes I saw Thief stepping in front of the lead horse and bringing the others to a halt. "They broke you in that Grove when they made you a Spear, Coriko. They broke you, but not beyond healing. I know your heart. I have been silent for three days because I believed that what we left behind in Grassland was truly behind us—that there would be no more killing. We found my home, our home, a place of peace. But it was not a place of peace, and the evils of Grassland came back."

There was nothing to say.

"So, I have decided this: you must promise me something. You must tell me that *with all your heart* you will try to not kill, *as long as you have strength in your hands.*"

I looked at Pippa, who now stood taller, wiser, than ever before. "With all my heart and with all the strength in my hands, I will try."

She pulled me to her.

"Oh, thank God," Father sighed.

Not long after, we spotted a horseman. It was a young churchman, his face red from the chill, who made his way up to our exhausted group. "Peace, Father! We have been expecting you!"

"Expecting us?" Father leaned forward. "How can that be, Brother? We had taken pains not to be seen."

"A messenger on horseback arrived this morning to say that soldiers were gathering at Berge. He stopped by your village on the way here to warn you. When he found it deserted he started after your trail, but soon stopped because of the mud. He needed speed and took the main road. We expect the army here in less than two weeks. Rokhan himself is coming. What has happened? Father Bergoin is anxious."

Father reached up to clasp the other churchman's hand. "In good time, Brother. We are all weary, and there are a number among us who are sick."

The horseman nodded. "I'll lead you into Gotten. There is hot water and a dry place to sleep. Father Bergoin has cleared the church of benches."

"Bless him!" Father opened his arms wide.

"Did you hear that, Thief?" Bran pounded his shoulder. "Hot water and sleeeeeeep!"

"Sleeeeeep!" Thief breathed. Together we looked behind, at the torn-up road, and the emptiness that would soon be filled with the sounds of jingling harness and creaking armor.

. . .

When the town of Gotten came into view we halted. The road widened long before the gate to form a clear swath, large enough to allow many people and animals to walk side by side. Stone walls spread out from a large metal gate, surrounding the dwellings, whose tiny roofs peeked out like children behind their mother. A tower stood at the southeast corner.

"Not as strong as a mountain," I muttered.

Thief frowned. "Better than the last place. I like the walls and the tower. We could fight from those places. Marumuk would like it."

The mention of Marumuk gave me courage. He had fought against this Outside army before, and although the Spears had lost much during that last battle before we escaped, they had lived, rebuilt, and taken control of the mountain again.

Just like Father's building, the church stood apart from the other structures, occupying the greater part of the western wall. I stared at its height, the tall arching roofs, and the shiny glass. "This is greater than the buildings of the old Spear village," I whispered to Pippa.

"Yes. Probably older too."

A large number of brown-cloaked men met us at the gate and reached to take burdens from the young and old. Frieda and the smaller children lay down near the fire in the large hall of the church, some falling asleep before the rest had even entered. Everywhere I looked, travelers leaned against walls, or lay on the stone floor. My eyes roamed the pictures that covered the church.

"Come, Pippa! Coriko. Bring your Thief and Feelah too," Father called. "This way, Bran. We must present ourselves to Father Bergoin." I glanced longingly at the fire before following the others to a quiet chamber at the side of the great hall.

The aged leader of Gotten, older than Father, regarded each of us with intelligent eyes. I felt him searching me, weighing my appearance, and anticipating the reasons we had come to his town. Yet, like Pippa's father, there was something about him that commanded trust.

"Welcome, Brother." His tone was measured and he tapped his lip thoughtfully. "You have come a long way." His gaze lingered on Thief and Feelah, though not unkindly.

71

Father made a little bow. "Father Bergoin. We thank you for your gracious hospitality. We are most grateful."

Bergoin nodded. "Yet the occasion for your arrival is unknown to us."

Pippa's father took a long look around him before he began. "Three nights ago our village was attacked by seven soldiers. One of them was Rokhan's cousin. They imprisoned us in the church and lit firebrands, ready to burn us alive. They gave no reason for their provocation other than, perhaps, too much ale. With the help of these young people, we were freed." He cleared his throat before adding, "Three of the soldiers were killed."

"Killed?"

"Two with arrows and one with the sword."

"By whose hand, Brother?" The question held no malice, yet I could feel the tension between the two men.

"By mine." I stepped forward. "And his." I pointed to Thief.

The eyes turned to me. "And who are you?"

"His name," Father answered, "is Coriko. My daughter—"

"Your daughter?" the older man raised his eyebrows. "I thought your family—"

Father cleared his throat. "She was dead to me, for all purposes. As you know, she was taken as a young child. She has returned in these last few days with her friends." He indicated all of us. "From across the sea!"

"Across the sea." The old man tapped his lip with more urgency. He glanced at an attendant, who raised his eyebrows knowingly. "Strange, don't you think, that we should hear about children from across the sea twice in a short time."

"God's ways," Father answered, raising a hand to the sky.

"God's ways, yes." Bergoin stared at the sword at my side, then at my clothes. He smiled at Pippa.

"Your daughter?"

"Yes. She is called Pippa."

"You are beautiful, child."

Pippa blushed. "Thank you."

"And blessed, with the powers of heaven, to be back with your father." He looked again at Thief and Feelah.

"I have not known of any to escape from those particular raiders before. There is a story behind each of you worth hearing, no doubt."

I shifted my feet. "Can this town be defended? We do not have long before Rokhan brings his soldiers."

The older man sank back against his chair. "A young warrior. And skillful with a *sword*, I'm sure."

I stiffened. Why had he used those words?

"This, my young soldier," he continued, "is a small town. There are no warriors here. Gotten is built and maintained on faith. It is true, we have financial . . . arrangements . . . with the conquerors. Arrangements that have kept us relatively unscathed." At my look of surprise he added, "Like the other towns along the coast, we have to pay off the marauders each year. But, truly, if you were to ask anyone within these walls, you would learn quickly that we place little hope in defenses or money. We pray, and we hope."

Pippa's father sighed. "There was nothing else for us to do, Father Bergoin, other than to come here."

"You have done no wrong, Brother," Bergoin affirmed. "These are your charges and you have brought them to the safest place available. God does not frown at you and neither do I. We will see what recompense we can raise."

"Thank you."

"What will they do?" I asked. "The Outside soldiers, what will they do if they come?"

"Outside?" Father Bergoin repeated.

"Our word for them. You would call them Rokhan's army."

"What they *want* to do and what they will be permitted to do are often different things," the old churchman answered. "Do not forget God, child."

"If they are permitted, will they kill everyone?" Pippa's words echoed in the large hall.

Bergoin half closed his eyes. "If they do not accept money, I fear they will turn the road red with blood."

I felt the sudden chill of battle creep into my chest. "Then we must leave immediately. It was a mistake to come here. There is no 'permission' with armies. I have seen what these soldiers do."

"A mistake?" Bergoin repeated. "I have lived long enough to recognize a poor choice. This was not one of them. No, my young warrior, I would say that you have been brought here for this very purpose. How it will be lived out, I do not know."

I stared at him blankly. What did he mean by that? Even Thief sensed something was strange and shuffled nervously.

"It seems to me," Bergoin continued, "that now would be a good time to hear your story. Any decision this important requires informed counsel. It is time for your tale. Let us see what gaps there are to fill."

"What we need is an army," Bran grumbled. "Our own army."

"We have no army. Our king was forced into exile three years ago, and we have not seen him since," Bergoin answered. "Rokhan—the king of Outside, as you call them—would say that *he* is lord of our lands. I imagine he comes to remind us of that now. Come, Pippa. It is time to hear what you would say to us."

I reached for a steaming mug from one of the churchmen. Pippa sipped from her own cup before speaking. "For the last nine summers we have been held captive by a people known as the Spears. They are an old culture, originally from somewhere to the north."

"I am aware of them," the churchman murmured. "There is not a village on the coast that has not been affected by their raids in one way or another. Strange that you should mention them when they have recently made contact with us."

Pippa reached for the table to steady herself. "They were here *too*?" she said. "And why do you say 'made contact'?"

"They were not raiding this time. They brought a letter. In a northern dialect."

He turned to the attendant at his side. "Brother, would you kindly retrieve the letter from my desk . . . and the shawl at my bench. The draft plagues me harshly this day." He folded his hands on the table. "Daughter, I pray you, continue. The contents of the correspondence will be shown soon enough."

Swallowing, Pippa tried again. "They . . . the Spears, live across the water, in the heart of a mountain, protected by the sea and the desert. We lived as slaves there, gathering shards that were taken by the Spears and turned into weapons. Thief and Feelah were slaves with us in Grassland." She nodded at our friends. "Some time later, two summers ago, Bran and his sister, Tia, were taken from their village and brought to Grassland. They had only been with us a few days when the Outside army attacked our mountain."

Father Bergoin nodded at her to go on. "These same soldiers have been plundering your villages," Pippa said. "Tia, Bran's older sister, was our leader. With her help, we escaped—most of us—until we were recaptured by the Spears many days later. The boys"—she indicated Thief and me—"were taken away from us and trained as Spears. We call this the Separation, the separating of mates."

Father Bergoin's eyebrows rose even higher.

"The girls were all taken to the mountain again," Pippa continued. "But this time, to learn the ways of the Spears. Tia, Bran's sister, fell in love with Marumuk, the leader of the Spears. She remained behind when we left."

Bergoin frowned. "As his . . . *mate?*"

"Yes—but do not think that by marrying him she is blindly following the Spear ways. She actually helped us to leave. She convinced Marumuk to let us go freely."

"Ah. The gaps are filling," he said mysteriously. At

78

that moment the attendant returned carrying a weathered piece of parchment.

"Timely." He nodded thanks to the attendant. "Child," he said, holding the paper out to Pippa, "I will guess that you can read. We were asked to give this letter to a group of children, should they come to our town; two boys who could handle swords, and two girls, one dark-haired, the other with hair the color of the sun." He smiled. "I do not doubt I am now looking at the proper recipients."

The paper shook in Pippa's hand. She scanned the words, then looked up at me in shock. "It is from Tia."

"Read it, Pippa," I urged. "What does it say?"

She nodded, and began. *"My dearest Pippa, Coriko, Feelah, and my Thief: Peace to you from Grassland."*

I shivered.

"Beyond all hope, I write this to you." Pippa looked up again. "Tia wrote this two seasons ago. It is nearing four seasons since we left Grassland. So Tia must have sent this in hope of her letter finding us, but not knowing when it might reach us." She went on. *"Your absence pains me each day, and all the more as I think of my brother."*

Bran winced and looked at the floor.

79

"*I write to you in desperation and haste. I know that I have no right to make my request, my friends, for I know firsthand what you have suffered. And yet I must. I ask you to return to me.*"

My thoughts spun in disbelief.

"*Many changes have taken place in Grassland since you left. You know Marumuk to be a strong leader, but I can now tell you that he is wise as well. He has heard my counsel about reforming the Spear culture, and as he can, he is effecting some of those changes. Those who dig the shards are no longer slaves. Our wealth from trading the shards is now shared more equally. And there is more that I have no time to tell you of here. It gladdens my heart that these changes are happening.*"
Pippa looked up to see if I had heard her. I nodded at her to go on. "*But they are not popular with all the Spears.*

"*A traitor has arisen in Grassland, one who deceives others in secret and is trying to take the leadership from Marumuk. At first we thought it was one of the Masters, but as time has gone on it appears that most of the dissension is coming from the Red Fists. Rezah believes this as well and has become my eyes and ears among the younger Spears. Even worse is what happened ten days ago. On a march to the village, Marumuk was struck by an arrow from an unseen attacker in the woods. The arrow was a Spear arrow."*

"Cowards!" I growled.

"My lord is healing well, but the time away from the leaders is seen as a weakness. We still control the army, but I am in terrible fear. I fear for Marumuk, and I fear . . ."

Pippa looked up from the parchment. *". . . and I fear for the child who now grows inside me."*

"A child!" I whispered.

"A baby," Bran echoed.

Thief took a step toward me, seeing the wonder on my face.

"Peace." I raised my hand. "Feelah? Can you explain to Thief as best you can? We will tell him everything once we have heard the rest."

Pippa continued. *"Unless you return to show good faith in Marumuk and strengthen our position among the young Red Fists, it will not be long, I think, before an untimely end comes to both of us."* In the pause that followed I could feel Pippa's fear. There was more. *"The story of your escape has grown since you left—told and retold again at firesides above and below the mountain. You are regarded as mighty warriors and leaders among both those who love and those who hate Marumuk. They recall how none could defeat Coriko and Thief in the Grove where the Red Fists trained. The young men remember you and look up to your skills, even if they resent your leaving.*

"Even old Mira tells the people that Pippa is a seer and Feelah a master of language." Feelah smiled at me. While Mira's strange ways had frightened me when I first met her in the mountain, I had come to respect her wisdom as an elder. *"Your names are mysterious and powerful in Grassland. Your swords and wisdom are needed again. I implore you to come to Marumuk's aid and to stand beside him. If there is strength at Marumuk's side, much bloodshed might be avoided.*

"I know that there is little hope of this letter finding you, but my heart feels the better knowing it has been sent. Copies of this letter travel to wherever the Spears make trade. Where once the orange sails were a sign of danger, Pippa will be happy to know that they are becoming a symbol of trade." Pippa smiled at me, then went on.

"*The raiding for slaves has stopped. This is another reason some of the Spears blame Marumuk, saying he is weak to trade rather than take.*"

Disbelieving, I asked, "Why would anyone trade with the Spears?"

"Merchants will sell to anyone who pays," Father Bergoin answered. "It is the nature of business. But please continue, Pippa."

"*Nonetheless, I pray you may be where our ships land, and that you are finally safe. Peace to each of you. Tia.*" As Pippa finished, a long silence filled the hall.

Bran was the first to speak. "I have to go. I have to go to Tia."

I looked at Thief's face as Feelah told him what the letter said. Then to Pippa. She was reading the letter over again, wonder filling her face.

"You can't go back!" I said to Bran. "None of us can. Ever."

"She is my sister—"

"Who thinks you are dead. As *we* will be dead, if we go back."

Feelah stepped forward. "I will hear what Pippa says."

"Of course we have to go back." Pippa lowered the message.

"Why are we even talking like this?" I looked to Bran for support.

But Pippa just carried on. "And Bran was right . . . we do need an army."

"Pippa?"

She held the letter out to Father Bergoin. "We have to go back to Grassland. To save our friend and to save her new child."

He watched her steadily, no less surprised than the rest of us at her next words.

"Coriko, there is more to this than any of us could have imagined. Tia says here that she has sent messages to towns in many ports and not one has reached us . . . until now. Is it *chance* alone that her words should reach us at the very place that the Outsiders' wrath will fall the hardest? Is it *chance* that Marumuk's time of need has come at the same hour as our own? No! It is not! The timing of all these things tells my heart there is no other choice but to return to the land of slavery. For in returning there we shall find the means to set ourselves free." She held the paper high in the great hall and all eyes were fixed on her. "And surely, in this of all places, a house of faith, we can make a choice of faith. It may not be the road we want to travel. But it is the path that will bring about peace for many."

The letter flapped in a sudden gust from the fire.

"What are you saying, child?" Father Bergoin asked.

"If we had an army," Pippa's voice grew louder, "the Outsiders would have to think twice before attacking this town. With an army standing on the walls of Gotten, they may well turn back and return no more. Ever. If there is a hope of stopping the bloodshed, then this is the path we must take."

Bergoin said nothing. Strangely, his focus was on me.

"Pippa," I said, "there is no army in this land other than the one coming for us!"

She nodded. "True. But *we* know where there is a very large army."

Bran moved up to us, watching Pippa eagerly.

"And we know the wife of their leader!" Pippa finished.

I shook my head. "Pippa, that is an impossible idea."

"Maybe not," Bran whispered.

"Even if we made it back to Grassland, how could we convince Marumuk . . . How could we convince them to come here?" I asked. "We were lucky to leave the first time."

She turned to me. "Do you still believe that? After all we have been through, you believe it was *good fortune* that brought us out from slavery?"

I wiped a trickle of sweat from my forehead. "No, I am not saying that." I stared at the arching ceiling. It was hard to argue when she became so determined. I needed words. "Tia needs time, Pippa. It is too soon to return and demand help. They are in enough trouble without us. She is asking for *our* help. How can we ask for *theirs*?"

Bran interrupted me. "None of us would be standing here if it were not for my sister. She saved you. How can we not help her?"

"And how can we receive help ourselves if we do not ask?" Pippa added.

Our words echoed in that great place and the frenzied drafts gusted as haphazardly as my thoughts.

"We have little time to think before a large army arrives here and wipes out two towns. Our best plan is to escape down the coast as quickly as we can," I said.

A determined look had settled on Pippa's face. "And what about all the little ones? The old, who cannot travel? Will we let them face the Outside army alone? And what about Tia?"

"I want to help Tia as well." Again, Feelah supported Pippa.

I turned to Thief. "Has Feelah told you everything? What do you think?"

He nodded. "I think I am going to die if I stay here and I think I am going to die if I go. Either way, I think I am going to die."

I groaned.

My friend grew more serious. "Look at her, Coriko. Look at Pippa. Look at my Feelah. When their hearts are set, what does it matter what we *think*? We have spent almost four seasons tromping this cold land because your Pippa tells us to . . . and Feelah agrees with her!"

Bergoin had remained mostly silent throughout our argument. Now he sat forward and spoke to Pippa. "Child, your faith is commendable. It is clear that you follow in the footsteps of your father."

"We *still* had to escape Grassland, Pippa," I said,

ignoring him. "Remember that. Tia saved us. At the risk of her own life."

"Yes, but Marumuk let us go *because* of her," Pippa countered. "Because he loves her."

"That does not mean he would come to help *us*," I answered.

Pippa turned to her father, then glanced at Bergoin. "I think he will," she whispered. "I know he will help. He needs us. Tia has asked us to come back."

Bergoin drew in a breath and exhaled slowly. "*This* is the army you are thinking of? An army that captured children and made them slaves?"

"Yes," Pippa murmured. "But there is change at the heart of that mountain, Father Bergoin, a change away from slavery, and it started with Tia. Grassland will be different if we return. Even when we left I sensed the beginnings of new paths. This must be why there is a challenge to Marumuk's leadership. Making alliances and coming out of hiding is not the usual way of the Spears. But it offers more than what the old ways can give. Grassland was cut to the heart when Outside came. Even though Marumuk saved it from complete destruction, it has taken so long to rebuild what Outside stole in one night. Marumuk has studied his enemies and watched the world unlike any Spear before him. If the Spears extend their trust to us, to this town, and later to others, there will be no going back to old ways. But there *will* be fewer secrets and more openness, more trade. More peace and less fear. Tia believes this. She just did not know how strong the challenge would be and who it would come from."

I smiled. Bergoin was not a fool. He could see the impossibility of it all. He would tell us to leave quickly with as many as we could, and find a safe place to hide until the Outside army went away.

The older man slid his gaze to Pippa's father. "What do you think, Brother?"

Father closed his eyes briefly. When he opened them again he put his hand on his daughter's head. "Pippa's faith is deep. I believe every word. Further, if it is your command, I will go to Grassland with them."

Bergoin shook his head. "I will not command anyone to go. As I said before, we live by faith in this community." He tapped the table. "If it is in your heart, Pippa, to go back in order to save your friend, and in so doing,

89

come back to save our people, I will not be the one to stop you. It may very well be that you have been brought here for this purpose."

"Madness!" I threw up my hands. "This is madness. You send us to our deaths and on a hopeless cause. Why lose everyone when we could all flee this place?"

The churchman shook his head. "I have seen an enemy much bigger than the one we face now. Worse than an army. A plague came over the land. It could not be run from, nor was there any place to hide. It came through our gates without any of us knowing or being able to do anything about it. Boils broke out on the people, and death followed." He rolled back his sleeve to reveal a number of small scars. "And then we prayed. Every last living soul prayed."

I stared at his arms in horror.

"And the plague stopped. I was in the path of that monster. Yet here I am."

Words caught on my tongue as I stared at the ugly scars. I swallowed. "Even if Marumuk agrees to Pippa's plan and sends an army to defend us, how can we bring them back with us before Outside gets here? It is days of travel."

"I do not see distance as an obstacle," Father Bergoin answered. "This is a town of sailors, and their fathers were sailors before them. We know the sea. The men of this town even know the coast that these Spears come from. Their trading ships have been seen frequently in the south, across the water. What they continue to hide is their exact location. I daresay no one is eager to sail too close to their land, despite their recent show of good will."

Pippa stared, hope filling her face.

Bergoin continued. "It takes time to bring as reckless an army as Rokhan's. His men are not organized like your Spears. They will burn and pillage all along the road. As evil as it is, pillaging takes considerable effort, and takes the soldiers' time when they would otherwise be traveling. I should say that you have two weeks, no more, before the city is besieged." He drew in a breath. "And it may be that Rokhan will listen to a truce."

I shook my head. "Marumuk took great pains to hide us from everyone. No ships sailed outside the bay except at night after the Outside left. The army stayed in the forest, not standing tall on the mountain waving flags. He is not ready to show the world the power of the Spears."

"You know that's not true." Pippa smiled. "The village was almost ready, the army was strong, and Marumuk was ready to face the Outside army. He even asked you to be a part of it. Your heart longs to make peace with him. You have carried the burden of his disappointment heavily, Coriko. Standing side by side with Marumuk, Tia's Marumuk, would heal a wound that cannot be mended any other way."

Her words stung. My old master had indeed asked me to help him build Grassland into something greater than what it had been before. A home . . . safety . . . food . . . Pippa in beautiful clothes—all these things we could have had. I thought of my friend Rezah, who stayed behind. And the treacherous Hammoth who betrayed us. They had everything they wanted in Grassland, while we had sailed, half starved, up and down the northern coasts as seasons came and went, searching for Pippa's home. But we left because Tia had not yet gained enough authority to make changes in Grassland. And short time or long, we feared we might eventually have been told to do the very things we were running from.

"It is hard for me," I said quietly to Pippa, "to hear words of war from your mouth."

She twirled a strand of her braid and for the briefest moment I thought she was going to suck on it as she used to when we were little. "I believe we can do this without spilling blood. And I believe it will be the saving of Grassland from falling forever into the evil it once was." She shivered. "I cannot feel that far ahead. I only know that Tia's message . . . and our coming to the village at just the right moment . . ." Her gaze flickered to the ceiling and the walls around us. "This faith-built town . . . Corki, now is the time for us to do things greater than we could imagine. I believe it is the right choice, and somehow it is better than running away. How I want you to believe this as I do!"

Meeting her gaze, I felt her longing, her hopes, and the strength of her faith that had guided us out of the mountain. I sighed deeply.

Bran brushed past my arm to stand beside her. "I will go with you, Pippa. I wish to see my sister again. And her child." He looked from Pippa to me. "Whatever the cost."

"Don't say that so quickly," I shot back. "There are some prices too high to pay. Would you see Tia only to lose Thief and me in a battle? Would you travel all the way to the mountain only to be stopped from seeing your sister?" I thought of Bergoin's scarred arms and of my Pippa, who looked so small, her little frame casting a tiny shadow across the table. "I will go back to Grassland trusting that Pippa's choice is right, and that we must once again walk the same path as the Spears." I took her hand. "You have been right so often before and never have I seen you so certain. But I will go with my sword loose in its scabbard, ready to fight, and ready to run. For all hangs on Marumuk's willingness to help us. I can think of no one stronger than Marumuk to save this town and our own lives as well. Thief and I know what the Spears can do. But will he *help* us?"

I turned to Bergoin. "Now would be a good time for all your people to pray! We are going back to Grassland. And for all the foolishness in the world—to ask Marumuk to bring his army here."

5

THE WIND BLEW MERCILESSLY AS our ship made its way out of Gotten's fjord. I kept my eyes fastened on the captain. He was focused on the rocks, heedless of the cold that whipped his cloak. His face was as clouded as the sky.

"Hold up oars!" he roared. "Bring her hard to starboard!" Fourteen men, already sweating in the icy air, bent their backs at the oars. I stumbled as the ship's deck suddenly sloped. Spray blasted off rocks only half a spear's throw away. "Bring her round," he yelled again. "Steady, tiller!"

The sail filled to bursting the moment we came free of the fjord and we shot ahead into open sea. How different it was to be in a boat where the men had volunteered to go—not forced into training as Thief and I had been after the Separation. These sailors were not bound by an oath as we were, nor were they watched by seasoned warriors to make sure they did as they were told. Father Bergoin had gathered a crew before the day was out, and provisions seemed to come from every direction.

It was a fast ship, and the crew moved with skillful ease. The oars were brought in and each man was busy with sails and rope and wood.

"Sailing at the end of winter," the captain muttered just loud enough for me to hear. "No one in his right mind sails in storm season. Ill luck, that's what these newcomers are." I stared nervously at the waves.

Father Bergoin had tried to calm my concerns about the captain before going aboard. "Do not mind the captain, Coriko," he said quietly. "He speaks of darkness on the brightest day and of drowning when he stands safe on the shore. It is his way of living with the sea." He caught my eye. "Yet there is none like him. If I were under his authority, I would trust him with my life. His sailors do."

Pippa and Feelah lay wrapped in warm skins, their heads hardly visible. Thief and Bran were hurling pebbles at sea birds swooping near the bow. The sailors raised a second sail. Together, the men looked as ragged as the Outside soldiers. The difference was that these men were skinny and did not look as if they would know what to do with a sword. I groaned silently. *Maker help us if we were attacked at sea.*

"They have good hearts, Coriko," Father whispered, as if knowing my thoughts. "Our coming to Gotten has put them in more danger than before, yet they sail willingly because they know the hope of all Gotten lies in the success of our voyage. But they are sailors and fishermen, nothing more. They will look to us for all things military."

"Then pray we meet no enemies, Father."

Even with the furs piled high about them, both girls looked chilled to the bone. "At least we are moving quickly on our journey to Grassland," Pippa said through chattering teeth. "Not like our slow sailing to find my village."

"I am going to bring the sun back with me," Feelah groaned.

"Stay warm," I said. "It will be cold until we sail farther south."

It was not long before the captain asked Bran to stand with him at the bow. Of all of us, Bran had the best sense of the sea. His father had often taken him and Tia fishing.

They held a large map between them, holding its edges against the wind.

"This is a wasted effort," I said.

Thief shrugged. "They seem to know each other's mind."

Bran pointed and waved until the captain finally sighed and nodded his agreement.

"For now," I answered.

My friend clapped me on the shoulder. "At least we are not those poor church people back there, waiting for Outside to arrive at their gate."

The wind blew hard all day until the light gave way to coming darkness.

When I crawled in beside Pippa and the others I was scolded. "Close the wraps, it's cold!"

Five of us huddled and tried to sleep as the night deepened. Father rested somewhere near, although when I had left him he was still talking with the captain.

"I am glad the children are not with us," Pippa whispered some time later. "I hope they are warm."

"They are safe beside the fire in Father Bergoin's church," I reminded her.

She rested her head on my shoulder. "Thank you," she said.

"Why?"

"Because you are here. Even though you do not think this is the right thing to do, you are here."

"Humph."

"Be quiet, you two," Bran grumbled.

I drifted asleep to the sound of waves slapping the hull and with Pippa's warm hand fast in my own.

In three days of sailing south, the cold eased and the girls came out from their wraps to walk on the deck.

"Much better." Feelah tilted her face to the sky. "My bones do not chatter anymore."

More than anything, the warmer weather gave us the chance to think clearly about what we were going to do when we arrived at Grassland.

"The difficult part," Feelah said, "is how can we get

to Tia?" Five of us were leaning on the starboard railing, watching the water foam against the hull. "Even if we reach the Spear village, how can we find her without being stuck with arrows?"

"Perhaps we should go to the mountain first," Pippa suggested. "She may be there."

Thief's eyebrows narrowed.

"Difficult." Feelah shook her head. "It was hard enough getting *out*. I do not think we could get back into the mountain safely. What if rebel Spears get to us first? And what if Tia or Marumuk was not there? We could remain captive for days without her even knowing. Or worse!"

"Does Marumuk know about her letter, I wonder?" Bran asked. "What if she didn't tell him? He wouldn't know we had been asked to come back."

"He must know," I answered. "He would not let ships go without his authority. But even if a small group of Spears were working on her orders only, I still think we will be allowed to speak, if we can get close enough to him or Tia."

"What if we found the tunnel—the one that Tia

showed us the first time?" Feelah suggested. "We could use it to get back into the mountain, look around, then come out again to the village if she was not there."

I groaned. "Why was this problem not thought through before we left? This whole plan is foolish."

"We do not even know who will meet us first," Bran added. "It could be, as Feelah says, that we are met by a part of the army that does not want us back."

Thief and I exchanged glances. "That would be the worst."

Feelah shrugged. "We could walk up to the village and say, 'Greetings! Where is Tia? We want to take her army home with us.'"

Thief laughed.

I groaned again.

"Wait!" Pippa gripped the railing. Her eyes were screwed up tight. "She is right. Feelah is right. That is what we must do." She opened her eyes slowly and looked at each of us. "We must give ourselves up to them and ask to see Tia."

Thief stopped laughing.

"There is no sense in that, Pippa." I measured my

words carefully. "The Spears are trained to destroy any who come near the mountain or the village. Remember the Strays? The Spears did not try to capture them. The only reason we were saved was because Thief and I were wearing helmets and capes. The Spears recognized us as their own."

"I do not think that we will find things the way we left them," Pippa replied.

"They will always be soldiers, Pippa," Thief argued. "It is in their blood."

She nodded. "Yes, even Tia believes in keeping an army. Marumuk has shown her that. But she will strive to stop the dark ways of the Spears. The raids, stealing children to work in the fields . . . these, I think, she will make a part of their past, not their new life as a people."

Thief threw his arm around Feelah's shoulders. "Pray you are right, Pippa. Or we will end up with arrows in our backs before we have reached the mountain."

Feelah thrust his arm away. "The Spears have changed!"

But would they have changed enough, I wondered.

Bran's eyes were red from staring into the wind and

from lack of sleep. "The captain says we are making our way faster than he had hoped. The wind blows with us." He looked at Pippa. "I need a braid. The wind keeps sending my hair into my eyes." They sat on the deck and Pippa began to braid his hair. The rest of us joined them to get out of the wind.

Bran's face darkened. He flicked his eyes toward the captain. "He is worried, Coriko. Worried that the speed that is bringing us to Grassland will be against us on the way home." He sighed. "Although he does not say it, I think he fears we will not get back in time to save the town."

Pippa stopped braiding. I blanched.

Feelah punched the side of my arm. "Why do you worry about such things? Our foolish plan is to walk up to the Spears and let them take us captive." She smiled. "And you are going to worry about the wind on the way home?"

On the fourth morning I woke to find Bran staring out to sea with his hands cupped to shade his eyes from the rising sun. "That is Grassland," he said solemnly.

I got up slowly, shaking off sleep. The mountain rose

unmistakably in the distance. "Yes, Bran is right."

The captain grunted, seemingly satisfied, and turned to the crew. "Make the ship ready for landing! All eyes watch for orange sails."

Father stretched in the morning light. "Well done, Bran. You have helped bring us here." He gazed at the new morning and cast off the cloak thrown loosely around his shoulders. "Look at those trees! It is a beautiful place, daughter," he said to Pippa. "How painful that they should destroy its beauty with the evils that have been done here." Sweat streamed from his face. "God be praised that at least you could not freeze in such a prison!"

And then the mountain's face came into view. The familiar grinning skull seemed to taunt, not welcome us.

"Can they see us from there?" Pippa asked.

"Yes."

"They will have seen us a long time ago," Thief murmured. "Marumuk does not sleep without eyes looking across both the desert and the ocean."

"They will not attack unless we attempt to land," I said. "They wish to keep the harbor as secret as long as possible. And we are not a war vessel." The bay of Grassland opened in front of us. The beaches were deserted. Long ago they were filled with our own footprints as we tried to escape from the Strays. I wondered whether the wild Diggers who had chosen to remain in the woods would again threaten us.

"We should not go near the land until we pass the mountain's bay," I said to the captain. "Let them think we are passing, or provisioning at most. There is a large stream flowing from the forest beyond the bay where we can get to shore. They expect ships to land there."

"I thought we wanted them to capture us." Bran frowned.

I turned to Thief. "What do you think? The bay or the stream trees?"

He thought for a moment. "Stream trees. We do not want them to attack the ship. And it is better for only a few of us to go to Tia."

"Yes," Pippa agreed.

The captain grunted. "I cannot take the ship up a stream."

I nodded. "We do not mean you to. We will need your small boat to row in to the land. I only ask that you wait at the stream trees for one day. If we do not return by then

. . . you and your men will have fewer mouths to feed on the way home."

His bushy eyes narrowed. "And we will have to face an army waiting to take not only our food but our lives as well. Do not mock me, little soldier. I did not come here to leave with my hands empty. An army returns with us or there is no reason to return. Father Bergoin is not one to risk lives lightly. Do your task, and I will do mine." He swung around and bellowed for the small boat to be brought to the ship's side.

"Helmets and capes," I said to Thief. "I want the guards in the woods to see us as Spears first. They will have to think before striking." I took Pippa's shoulder and leaned close to her. "Now is the time for praying."

The captain blocked me as I made my way to the ship's side. "I have a wife. A son." He lowered his voice. "Do not come back without the help we need to keep them alive, little warrior. You have one day. You and your dreamer. And may God give you everything you need to succeed."

"We will be back, Captain," Pippa answered. She stepped around me and laid a hand on his arm. "With an army."

They held each other's stare for a moment before he pulled away to issue another order.

"His fear is great," Father said as the small boat was lowered. "And he speaks for others too, not just himself."

It was true. The sailors no longer hurried about the decks. Instead, they stared silently, each watching as one by one we disappeared over the side of their boat. Our task, I realized, held their future. I could still feel the captain's stare as Thief and Father began to heave on the oars of our small boat. As the beat of their rowing rose and fell with the waves, I found myself twisting to look back at the ship, at the figures pressed against the railings.

"How long would it take a troop to get from the village to the stream trees?" I asked Thief.

"Not long. But we should reach the beach before any large patrol arrives."

As we approached the sand my heart began to race. Would the Spears hold their arrows? It had not been a part of my training to give myself up. There was, I discovered, just as much risk in surrender as there was in escape. When the bow of our boat struck the beach it took all my strength not to draw my sword.

6

ONLY STEPS ONTO THE BEACH, Bran sensed danger. "Strays," he muttered, catching the edge of my cape. He sniffed. "They are close."

Father wrinkled his nose. "What are Strays?"

"They are wild children," Pippa answered. "They used to be with us in Grassland, as Diggers. But they left us when we escaped from the mountain. They lived for a while in the burned village until the Spears came again. They are dangerous and cunning."

The wind was changing, and a dreadful smell wafted toward us.

The sound of Thief's sword scraping from his scabbard caused me to pull my own. We stood side by side.

"Bran, what will they do?" I asked between clenched

teeth. The wind blew gently through the near trees and the sound of the rushing stream rose above the tide. Bran had once lived among the Strays. He would have some sense of what they might be planning.

Bran's hands were shaking. "They are all here, Coriko. All of them. We should get back in the boat."

"No!" I planted my feet firmly. "The Spears will be here soon. We cannot go back. This is where we must stand our ground."

Bran shook his head. "We can't! We should go back to the ship. There are too few of us. They are waiting for the signal to rush us. Please, let's go back. Now."

Feelah grabbed at Pippa. "Let us go. Let us go!"

"What do you want me to do?" Father called.

"I can smell them," Thief barked hoarsely.

I stiffened. The first figure suddenly appeared through the trees. He was more of a shadow than anything else, but I could see someone giving directions.

"Peace," I whispered to myself. "Balance the blade. Patience." I flicked my visor into place so that the eye-guards allowed me to see without hindrance. How strange it was, I thought, to be facing them all over again. The last time they found us near the beach they had chased us like animals through the woods. Not this time.

"Here they come," Bran moaned. He took a step back.

"Girls in the boat?" Thief whispered to me.

"Bran!" I did not look back over my shoulder. "Father. Get in the boat. Take the girls to safety."

"No, my son." I heard his heavy step on the sand. "I will stay."

"Pippa, get in the boat."

"No, Coriko."

The bushes nearest the sand began to rustle.

"There is strength in stone," Thief chanted.

"And two are stronger than one," I answered. Our swords were poised to strike.

"Mercy," Pippa prayed behind us. "Have mercy on all."

"And keep our hearts from hatred," her father joined in. He began to roll up his sleeves.

"What are you doing?" I asked through gritted teeth.

He finished one sleeve and turned to the other. Then he smiled, raising two meaty fists—fists that reminded me of a farmer I had faced on my first raid as a Spear. "I do not need sticks and stones," he said. "These have served me well enough in the past."

Thief held a dagger as well, switching his sword to his other hand. "They may hold off if one or two fall early," he muttered.

The Strays came from all directions, bursting from the woods and bushes like a herd of pigs. There was no yelling. Only the silence of hatred.

From the corners of my eyes I could see Thief's helmet tilted down, ready for battle on one side of me, and Father's determined scowl on the other. Many would fall while the three of us were still alive.

Before the first Strays reached us, a row of arrows suddenly appeared in the sand only strides from our feet. They sank into the beach one after the other, as if a farmer had sown neat furrows of grain. The Strays stopped abruptly. In that brief moment we stared at the Strays from behind the barrier of arrows. Filthy, wild faces looked back at us.

"They could use a wash," Father remarked. A tall boy with thick black hair snarled at me and raised his hands like claws.

He turned one of his hands into a fist and signed *death* at me. Thief roared back at him. Gnashing his teeth, the Stray jumped over the arrows. Before my sword could reach him Father's powerful hands caught him by the throat. He held the boy briefly with his feet dangling above the arrows before tossing him back to the sand.

"No closer, son," Father said, "or I'll have to knock you down again." Then to me he added. "Try to use the flat of your sword. These are children."

The boy spat at the churchman and bent his knees, ready to spring again.

An arrow ripped into the sand by the Stray's foot and he backed up. Another followed. Eyes wide in terror, the Stray scrambled to the safety of the trees.

"Corki!" Pippa shrieked. I whirled to find three Strays grappling with Bran.

In two strides I was beside him. I smacked the nearest boy on the side of the head with the flat of my sword and he fell. I rammed my helmet into the forehead of a second, and the third pulled away from Bran when he saw me brandish my sword. Several more arrows fell and the Strays began to run, watching the woods with terror.

Bran was breathing heavily.

I lifted his chin. "All is well?"

He nodded.

I turned to the girls.

"We are fine," Feelah answered. "A good thing they ran when they did," she growled. "I would not have been as merciful as you."

"You did not kill anyone," Pippa gasped.

My sword hand was still ringing from the blow I had given the Stray. I looked at the blade. For once, there was no blood.

The arrows at our feet looked far too familiar. I glanced at their likely flight path from the trees.

"The Spears are here."

Father wiped his brow. "Well, that wasn't much of a fight, was it?"

"Why did the Spears not kill?" Thief asked. "None of them would miss from this range. They could have taken all of us."

"Coriko?" Father asked. "What is happening?"

I did not turn my head. "The Spears are here, Father. In the woods, on either side."

"Ah," he said. "They are the ones who shot the arrows then?"

"Yes."

"Yet they have not killed us."

"No, they have not."

"I will take that as a good sign." He began to unroll his sleeves.

It was not long before the Spears stepped from the trees. There were ten of them, five on either side of the beach.

"Red Fists," Thief muttered. "No Masters with them." Two in each group had their bows aimed at us, ready to fire. Another walked backward, watching the retreating Strays. The troop on our right approached first. A soldier, no taller than any of us, stepped confidently toward me. I gasped in surprise. It was Rezah.

"Coriko." I could hear his smile beneath the mask.

"Rezah!" I grabbed his arm.

"And Thief too." He clapped my friend on the back and saluted the girls.

I shook my head in surprise. "I worried for you," I said. "The night you saved us . . . If you had not warned us—"

He cut off my words with his eyes—the other guards were too close. "I cannot believe my eyes." He lowered his voice. "You must have courage the size of the ocean to be here. Or your minds are unsteady."

Thief and I exchanged glances. "It could have been worse for us if it was not you, Rezah."

There was a quiet chuckle from the Red Fist. "Your ship was spotted last night on the watch. We saw you long before you landed." He leaned toward us. "You bring strange company, Coriko."

"Pippa's father," I answered. "The others on the ship come from a town near where she lives."

He nodded and did not ask any further questions.

"Why did you not kill the Strays, Rezah?"

He looked toward the trees. "You will not find the mountain as you left it, Coriko. Many changes have taken place in the time you have been away." He looked hard at me. "Many changes. We do not kill Strays anymore, unless we have to. Instead, they help disguise Grassland

115

from ships that pass by or stop for water near the bay. Tia says that Outside scouts will see the wild ones and think there is no one else here. She has a strong will, Coriko. And she is wise."

"What of Tia?" Bran asked.

"Peace, Bran," I said. "Patience."

"I want to go to her, now. She does not even know that I am alive."

"I know. But be patient."

A low whistle came from the trees.

"We must leave the open beach." Rezah signaled to the waiting Red Fists. "We will take you to Marumuk."

"What does Marumuk say of us?" I asked him.

He shrugged. "Marumuk says very little of anything these days. He is even more cautious than before with his words. I have heard Tia speak of you in front of him and he has shown nothing of his thinking one way or the other. But he thought it was you on this ship and he guessed rightly. Tia stands on watch each day, waiting for an answer to her letters. Rarely do strange ships harbor here, as there is fresh water near the stream trees. It is likely why I was sent."

I put my hand on his arm. "*Marumuk* sent you?"

He shook his head. "No. Tia did. But she does nothing without his approval."

Thief watched Rezah as he started for the trees. "What do you think?"

I shrugged. "I do not know. It is encouraging that Tia still has some power. But how much? And will it be enough?"

My friend grunted. "Keep your sword loose."

I could not stop a feeling of dread from sweeping over me at the sound of Marumuk's name. I could see from the discipline of Rezah's soldiers and their diligence to follow orders that some things had not changed. But the Spears did not take our weapons as I had expected. Instead, five Red Fists went in front of us, and five followed behind.

There was no speaking once we were under the trees. The Red Fists led us quickly, along paths I knew as well as any of them, from the days of our training in the Grove. How many other ways of the Spears remained the same? I could only hope that Tia would speak on our behalf and save us from the wrath of Marumuk.

Father hummed as he walked, noticing everything: the

birds, the trees, the clear blue sky. Pippa offered her hand to me. When she squeezed it, I sensed her excitement. Yet her palm was cold and I knew she was looking ahead to the mountain, where our lives and the survival of a whole town would hang in the balance.

Rezah led us away from the village and toward the mountain. I was surprised at first. Yet the more I walked, the more it made sense. The mountain had been the first home of the Spears, and it was the watchtower of Grassland. Marumuk had always used it for secret councils and plans.

Through the branches I glimpsed the stony walls of the mountain thrusting up from the forest floor. Soon the gaping mouth of a tunnel opened up ahead of us. The light of the forest gave way to the flickering shadows cast by torches stuck in the walls. I did not recognize it as any entrance we had used or seen. This was not surprising— the mountain held many tunnels for the Spears, and we had not been there long enough to learn all of them. I marched in unison with the guards, and with the tread of our feet came the memory of order, rules, discipline.

Pippa tugged at me. "Corki."

"Quiet, Pippa. We do not speak in the tunnels."

"*We* always did," she answered. "And you are not a Red Fist anymore."

I had forgotten that the girls had spent their training more in the mountain than anywhere else.

"I am afraid," she said.

"Why? We have been in tunnels all our lives. You should not fear darkness."

She breathed out slowly. "I am not afraid of *where* we are. It is something else. There is a weight on me that will not go away. Every time I sleep, I see the town of Gotten. It is as if I feel each child, each woman, each man, standing there, waiting for us to do something that will save them. It is too much to bear."

I did not answer at first.

"What if my heart is wrong, Corki, and Marumuk does not help us?"

"Do your dreams say that we fail on this journey?"

She shook her head. "It is not like that. I cannot see what lies ahead. I am simply given a sense of the path we should take."

"Then this is our path, Pippa. This is what you were

given. We cannot go back. We must do our task and go. Always, your praying has taken us to places of peace. It will again. And at least we bring a brother back to his sister."

She rested her head against my arm. "That is not something you would have said a while ago."

The words had come easily enough from my mouth, and I spoke them with good intent, but my heart raced as if I did not believe them. Behind us, Father's reassuring steps followed, confident and unfailing.

We journeyed upward, passing doors that led to other tunnels as we went. Finally Rezah came to a stop as the passage opened up to a large room. Daylight streamed onto the floor from a hole in the rock ceiling. It was warm, and the wall glistened with moisture.

"I know this chamber," Pippa whispered.

Feelah knew it as well. "We are near the Hall of Meeting," she whispered.

They took us along one more passage before stopping in front of a large door.

"This way," Rezah spoke softly. He stood beside the open door and his soldiers took their places along the tunnel wall. "Remove your helmets," he added.

I leaned up to him before I took mine off so that our foreheads touched. "I wish you could have come with us," I whispered.

His eyes flashed to the sides where the other guards stood in silence. "At least you have come back," he answered.

"I will not forget what you did for us, Rezah. You risked everything. You are a true friend."

He nodded quickly. "Trust no one! Only Tia and Marumuk. Traitors abound, though they are hidden by their masks. Avoid Hammoth most of all!"

"Hammoth!" I wanted to press Rezah more for information, but Pippa had gone inside. I followed her, straining to see ahead and wondering about Hammoth, the Red Fist who had betrayed our escape from this place.

I followed Pippa inside, straining to see over her shoulder. My chest was pounding and my mouth had gone dry. Instinctively, I felt for my sword. We did not have to wait.

The chamber was empty except for two figures seated by the fire. Tia looked more beautiful than I had remembered. Her long black hair hung freely over her pure white gown and she stood as we entered. The bulge at her stomach was unmistakable. Beside her, the powerful Marumuk fixed his gaze on me.

Tia gave a cry, and Pippa ran to her before I could stop her. Feelah was right behind Pippa. Thief and I stood awkwardly while Father returned Marumuk's stare with a smile.

"My boys!" Tia beckoned us. "My—" She stopped when her eyes fell on her brother. Her arms went limp around the girls' shoulders and they released her. Bran stood beside me, trembling.

"Bran!"

Brother and sister met in the center of the chamber, and we all watched silently as they wept together.

"You were dead!" Tia whispered.

"And you've become a leader!"

"You look so much like our father," she sobbed. Tia locked eyes with me. "How can so much good come in one day? Let this not be a dream."

"God be praised," Father murmured.

When the pair stood, the rest of us gathered and Tia hugged and kissed each of us in turn. Father remained where he was, near the door.

"My heart overflows," Tia said through her tears. Even

her eyes looked older to me now. Rezah was right. She had grown wise. Her hugs felt the same as they had when she led us from Grassland, but there was change in everything else. She was aware, I knew, of Marumuk, still seated behind us. "Come to the fire."

Her step faltered suddenly, and she reached out to steady herself. I took her arm.

"Thank you," she whispered. Her face had gone white. I looked questioningly at Pippa. She was staring intently at Tia. Approaching Marumuk, I desperately straightened my weather-beaten war cloak. However, it was Tia who broke the silence again. "I am almost undone at the sight of you," she began. She held on to Bran's hands while looking us over again for the twentieth time. She turned to Father. "I cannot find a proper thanks for bringing my brother to us," she said in the Northern tongue.

Then she turned back to us. "Beyond all hope, one of my messages reached you. I sent them in desperation, many of them—sometimes more for comfort at writing your names than anything else. I did not expect to see any of you again. Yet from your faces I think that neither Bran nor my letters are the only reason you are here." This time she looked at me.

I bowed to Marumuk. Even under Tia's encouraging gaze I could not help feeling like a small animal caught between the paws of its predator. How could I make peace with this man who felt so strongly that I had betrayed him? "There is another purpose for our coming." I used the Spear language. A thought swept through my mind, of Father, falling on his knees at the first sight of Pippa.

I dropped to my knees. I held out my sword. "But we do bring you these, that we may help Tia . . . if it is in our power."

Thief knelt beside me, drawing his sword. Marumuk watched us without expression. Words caught in my throat. I felt as if we were back in the Grove again, and the shame of running away washed over me anew.

"We have also come," Pippa said, coming to my aid, "to ask for your help."

Marumuk let out something like a growl.

Pippa swallowed. Her gaze shifted from Tia to Marumuk. "The man at the door is my father," she continued. "We have been to his village. Even as we speak, Rokhan, the king of Outside, together with the very army that attacked this mountain, is gathering to wipe them out. Everyone will be destroyed. You know the way of the Outside. There is no mercy with them. Blood will flow like water and there will be no children left to keep my father's town alive."

Marumuk finally spoke. "What is that to us?"

Pippa met his reproachful gaze. "I believe it does mean something to you."

At that moment Father came forward and put his hands on both our shoulders. Under his encouraging arms I dared to speak again. "We hoped that you might bring ships and come to their aid," I said.

Marumuk rose to his towering height. Tia watched every flicker in his face. "Do you think we are an army for *hire*?" He snorted. "Did you learn nothing of what I taught you? The army of Outside is our greatest enemy. I do not send our forces foolishly to shed their blood far from these shores." He looked at Tia. "It was a mistake to send the messages. I warned you of this. Hope is found in practice and precision, not dreams."

The chamber shook with his voice and rattled my hopes along with it. I cast my eyes down to the floor in despair. We were fools. Not only had we put our lives in danger, we had stolen precious time away from the people of Gotten.

"My lord." Tia released herself from Bran and took Marumuk's arm. "I beg your patience. Let us not miss an *opportunity* offered so freely to us—one not so easily seen at first glance."

Marumuk looked down at his wife.

She held a finger up, requesting his patience, then turned to Pippa. "Did you not say that Rokhan himself comes with the army?"

"Yes."

Tia smiled and turned back to Marumuk. "Then, my lord, there may be more in this venture for the Spears than our ears have heard."

"How so?" His great voice boomed.

Tia's eyes shone in the firelight. "Do we not have the power of surprise working for us? No Outsider would expect the Spears to help a small foreign village. None would dare imagine that the black capes from the 'deserted' mountain would be so rash—if they were even alive—to attack the power of Outside! Who would expect us to slip into Gotten as raiders at dawn? With the utmost care, my lord, we may have the chance to be rid of our greatest enemy forever."

7

EVERY EYE WAS FIXED ON TIA. The fire crackled and cast flickering shadows all the way to my feet.

"What do you mean?" Marumuk asked.

Tia tightened her grip on his arm. "My lord, if Rokhan has left his lair and stands openly with his men—"

Marumuk stopped her with a wave. "An arrow in his back? He is not a fool. He travels with his best guards. They surround him day and night. I have tried this route already."

Tia continued. "I do not mean for us to kill him." She paused. "In the North, the lords and kings frequently go to war in far countries. When prisoners are taken, wealthy knights who are captured are ransomed. Their families *buy* them back. I have heard stories of lords who were not returned to their lands for several years until the full sum was paid."

Pippa's eyes shone. "A hostage."

"Yes!" Tia nodded. "I mean for us to steal him, but not for money or trade."

"No," Pippa went on. "Bring him back here to the mountain, where he can send messages to remind his army that their king does not wish them to attack anyone. A bloodless war!"

Marumuk's gaze shifted in my direction.

I raised my eyebrows to show my interest, and because I was surprised that he wanted to know my opinion.

Tia pressed her point. "Rokhan's people believe, after all, that he is a son of the gods. He has led them successfully on every field of battle. They will not take his capture lightly."

Marumuk tugged at his lip. "It would be difficult."

Tia nodded. "Yes, but worth it. Imagine never having to fear the Outside again."

Marumuk's frown deepened. "In time they would choose a new king, Tia, even if they think of him as a god. What then?"

A thought suddenly struck me. "Then we would promise Rokhan the support he needs to fight the new king. Help him back to power among the Outsiders. Divide the strong and they become weak. You taught me that, Marumuk. We always attack in the dark, by surprise, when the powerful are resting and cannot unite quickly enough to mount a defense. If we confused the Outsiders by making them have to choose sides—the old king, or a new king—we could divide their forces. If he had to rely on the Spears, the old king would be forever in your debt."

Thief nodded. "They might even fight each other if we are lucky."

There was another long pause as Marumuk studied me. "And where will you be in all of this?"

The words were a weight, a ship's anchor on my heart. Pippa rested her hand on my shoulder, and I found new courage. "If the Spears agree to help Gotten, then they are truly changed. They are not people who brought only fear, as I once knew them. If this is the truth, then I will stand by Marumuk's side."

Marumuk said nothing. His eyes flickered to Thief.

"I stand with Coriko, and I will stand with you," my friend agreed.

Tia spoke again. "My lord, you have heard good advice! And most of all, what better way to unite all Spears? Destroy all hint of rebellion *here* by capturing our worst enemy, Rokhan. Standing at your side would be two returning warriors, Coriko and Thief, whose names are well known among our people. There could be peace, or at least a truce, between Outside and Grassland. Our ships could enter any harbor without reprisals. Workers could be paid and not stolen. We could plant the seeds for a reigning peace with the capture of one man!"

Turning away from all of us, Marumuk faced the fire. "Peace is an illusive dream. It comes with shadows at night. It brings flickers of hope while the darkness lasts. But in the morning it is gone, the shadows have fled and the fire has gone out."

Pippa stepped up to him, looking so small beside his great height. "In the caves of this mountain, Corki and I once lived as slaves. We talked about a place of peace every night. All around us was an army against whom we could not win. But we waited and watched and prayed. In time, we were given the chance to seek freedom and peace. We took it, against great odds."

Marumuk looked thoughtful.

"A way is being offered here, now," Pippa said. "A way full of questions and risk. But a way nonetheless."

"A way," Tia added, "for those with courage. Our reforms, Marumuk, have already raised doubt among some of the Spears. The murmuring complaints need to be quelled by action. Here is a chance for us to take. If we win, none will be able to speak against us."

There was a resounding silence.

Marumuk folded his arms. "Maybe so. But one question has not been answered. How will we steal the king of Outside? Rokhan does not easily leave himself open to attack. You know this, Tia."

Tia moved gracefully toward the fire, always watching her mate. "It seems, my lord, that we would need all of the skills you have given the Spears. Stealth, secrecy, speed like a fox." She stopped as she passed Thief. "And yet, I think more than anything, we would need a thief. One who can slip into the ranks of Outside, learn their thoughts, their intentions, their vulnerabilities. With a proper thief we could steal Rokhan and leave his army leaderless." For once, her eyes left Marumuk. "And we have such a thief."

Everyone turned to look at my friend.

"What?" Thief muttered.

Marumuk remained unmoved. "Leave us!" he ordered. "For a brief time only, while I consider your request."

I caught the eyes of each of my friends and left the room with Pippa's steps echoing close behind.

Food was brought to us in an airy chamber, and we sat in silence for some time.

"What will he do?" Thief broke the stillness.

"I hope, I hope . . ." Pippa murmured. Her hands were clasped in prayer.

"Difficult to say," I answered Thief. "Would *you* know what to do if you were Marumuk?"

Our food was long gone when the door to the chamber opened again. Tia's eyes shone in the torchlight. She smiled. "Make ready to leave for Gotten!"

The captain had a difficult time closing his mouth. Around the far headland, eight orange sails covered the sea, their dragon prows grinning evilly. Each boat held twelve men, with six shields hung on either side. Even closer, ten Spears now stood on our own deck, and the sailors frequently looked up from their duties to watch the impressive soldiers on guard. Capes billowed and hands rested on beautifully crafted swords as they faced the sea.

"I did not think . . ." the captain stammered. "I cannot believe . . ."

"Exactly," Father finished for him. "But you must try to. They will be following at your stern until we reach Gotten, and it would be a shame for you to remain an unbeliever for that long."

I tried to see the figures on the lead ship. One of them was Marumuk, for there was no one else as tall. The others were more difficult to see.

"She is there," Pippa assured us.

"Tia is different than she was just yesterday." I kept looking at the ship. "I think she is sick." I shielded my eyes and squinted. "And I cannot see her now."

"I do not think she will go unseen for long." Pippa smiled. "Despite Marumuk's wishes to leave her behind."

"What choice does he have?" I countered. "Tia made the plans. And he relies on her to help against unforeseen events. No plan is ever delivered without changes. Besides all that"—I grinned—"she is almost as stubborn as someone else I know."

"If you wish to kiss me again, Coriko," Pippa said, "I would use more caution with your words."

Bran remained with Tia on board Marumuk's lead ship. Although he had been needed to navigate our journey to Grassland, it took only a brief description for the Spears to know exactly where the town of Gotten lay.

Without a trace of a smile Marumuk had simply said, "We have been there before."

The wind was not as kind on our return trip. Frequently the captain had to call out orders to change sails in order for us to battle our way northward.

"Likely won't get there in time anyway," he grumbled. "Just as quickly lose half this little fleet to a storm, no doubt."

I faced the wind, willing it to turn about. If we fought the weather like this the whole way back, the Outside army would beat us to the town. As it was, we had only a few days to prepare for their coming. All our hopes lay in a thief, and there was nothing he could do until we reached Gotten.

On the second day of sailing from Grassland, Thief and I took a watch at the bow. Two orange sails kept pace with us on either side and the watchmen glanced in our direction from time to time. Although I slept throughout the night, a troubled dream began to grow with the morning.

"Eight ships." I kept my head below the gunwale and the wind. "Only eight." I sighed. "That makes a small army of just over a hundred Spears. How many men will Outside bring?"

Thief was trying to get the watchmen from the other ships to wave. He blew on his cold fingers. "It is better than none. I would stand with this group. They are excellent warriors."

"I have no doubt of their courage or skill," I answered. "It is their number. Outside almost destroyed Grassland. They are like the sand of a beach! How can we fight against so many?"

Thief shrugged and scratched his nose. "If all goes well, there will not be much need. It is not the fighting I am worried about. It is the other part of Tia's plan that turns my stomach."

"Do you think you can do it?"

"Will you go with me?"

"Yes."

He looked over his shoulder to amidships, where the girls had taken shelter from the chill. "Pippa will not want you to go."

"I know." I focused on the waves.

To my delight, Rezah had been assigned to our boat. He ate with us when he could and was given leave by his group's Master to sleep near us as well. He spoke of all the things that had happened in the mountain since we left.

"There has been no more talk of raids," he said one night. "We trade shards for the things we need. Or," he grinned, "we win them honestly in battle."

"And who will pick the shards, I wonder?" Pippa asked.

"There is rumor that Red Fists will take turns on guard and on the field. As more children are born to the Spears, each family will be responsible for bringing in shards. There is a large stock in the mountain still, so there is time. But these are the questions that some of those who disagree with Marumuk are asking."

"But the army is still strong." I pressed him to say more.

"Yes. Marumuk trains us as hard as ever. But he gives more freedom too. We see our mates regularly now. Our homes have been built, Coriko." He clapped my shoulder. "We live in our own homes! I would not leave now for anything. Even if it means that I must pick shards again."

As we drifted off to sleep that night, I thought of the beautiful homes Marumuk had shown us last winter, and told Pippa what Rezah had said.

"I would like a home for us too," she murmured.

I could only hope we would be alive long enough to have one. Again, my heart ached for a place where we could finally rest. I turned over to see Father standing patiently above us, watching the stars. The cold did not seem to bother him, and when the wind gusted, he flung his hood over his head.

"What do you think we will find when we get there,

Father?" I whispered. "Will the town be in fire and smoke?"

He blew out a long breath. "Did you even imagine we would make it this far? Did you believe that there would be an army behind us, no matter how small?"

"No. I did not."

"Then let us not worry too much about what awaits us. Let us rather expect help when we need it most."

Late in the night I awoke with a terrible thirst. Creeping out from under the furs, I sat up and made my way to the back of the ship. As I stepped toward the water barrels, my foot slipped on the icy deck and I bumped into the Red Fist standing watch.

"Forgive me," I muttered. "I slipped."

To my surprise, he pushed me back. "As any fool would," he answered.

His voice was familiar. "Hammoth!" I had kept a wary eye on him since setting sail, especially after Rezah's words, but this was the first time we had faced each other alone.

He stared back arrogantly, his Spear cape held out wide to make himself look bigger. I knew what he was doing—I had done the same thing many times before.

"I do not know why Marumuk wastes his time with traitors," he snarled. "It is not for me to decide. If it were, I would not be letting you take us on a fool's mission. You and your little thief."

Only wisdom kept me from knocking him off the edge of the boat. "If you were not under Marumuk's command, I would help you make friends with the fish."

"You grow weaker away from the Grove, traitor," he spat at me. "Perhaps even your pretty Pippa knows this. Pretty, pretty Pippa."

I hit him. I knew from experience that his stomach held the least protection and my fist landed solidly. He doubled over, wheezing.

"You are not worthy to even speak her name," I said.

"That will be paid for, Coriko," he snarled. "When you have an Outside arrow in your back, perhaps I will take her for myself. She would do better with me than with you."

I was about to kick him over the side when I was grabbed from behind.

"Go back, lad," Father said. "Lie down and cool down. I don't know what this is about, but an army divided is an army defeated. Go to sleep."

I allowed myself to be turned around. "Stay away from her, Hammoth," I whispered over my shoulder. "For your life's sake . . . stay away."

Chuckling quietly, he repositioned his spear. We both knew it was an even match. I had hit him without warning. With a weapon, he had the advantage. Yet he knew that my blood boiled and even if he struck me I would likely carry both of us into the sea.

"Stay away," I growled.

"Come on, lad." Father pushed me gently.

"Pretty, pretty," Hammoth crooned.

I shook Rezah awake. "Hammoth just challenged me. I went for water and he was on watch."

Rezah pulled his furs up higher. "Stay away from him, Coriko. He follows Marumuk's orders, but he has not forgotten your last meeting. He has many friends among the Spears, and the Masters look on him with favor."

"And Marumuk?" I asked.

"Marumuk has never liked him."

On the third and fourth days the weather changed. A black cloud rose up from the south, bringing with it a torrent of rain and wind at our backs. Night and day we were driven by the storm.

"Quite a breeze!" Father yelled above the tempest.

The captain nodded, and for the first time he looked satisfied. "It's a fair wind. We might even make it to the town before it is turned to rubble."

I threw up my meal into the sea.

On the morning of the fifth day the fjord of Gotten appeared in the gray light. A series of signals from Marumuk's flagship made our captain lower the sail.

"We will approach from the woods!" Marumuk shouted. "Do not enter the fjord. Follow."

The orange sail passed us, with the others falling into a line.

"Fancy sailing," the captain snarled. "But what is wrong with our harbor?"

"We cannot afford to be seen by scouts," I said to him.

"Hrmph!" he grunted, and bellowed for the sail to be raised again.

We landed on the northwest side of the town, with each ship skillfully sliding onto the beach. No sooner had the prows breached the rocky shore than the Spears leapt out. Our own ship let the anchor down, and it took three trips back and forth in the small boat to deliver all of us to shore. Everywhere I looked, black capes filled the sand, and dark helmets gleamed. Marumuk and Tia were hardly visible. Here we stood, in Gotten, and with us stood many experienced Spears, tall and wary. I would not have believed it possible when we left the town.

"We may just have a chance, Pippa," I told her.

"God help us," she whispered as we walked through the towering soldiers. As they parted for us I noticed others, busily chopping branches from the trees and hurling them onto the ships.

"What are they doing?" Pippa asked.

"Marumuk takes no chances." I smiled. "He is hiding his boats."

Tia greeted us warmly again. We had not spoken in five

days on board the ships, and it filled me with confidence to see her face.

"The Outside has not arrived yet," Tia said urgently.

"How do we know?"

"Scouts have been to the town and come back while you were unloading," Marumuk answered for her. "But even without their report, we would know. There is no smoke. With the Outside army, there is always burning from their pillaging. They cannot help themselves." He looked at Father. "Take us into the town. We are going to need the help of the churchmen."

We followed Father through the trees in a long line of sailors and soldiers. A small number, I noticed, remained with the boats. Only the glint of weapons told me that Spears were on guard, hidden beneath the branches that now covered the boats from prow to stern.

Feelah walked with clenched fists.

"He will be fine, Feelah," I said. "He is a good thief."

She brushed aside an angry tear. "Why do they need my Thief? Is there not a Spear that can do this?"

I took her hand. "I've seen him on a raid. Thief led us all into the house without getting caught. He found the room. He took his captive perfectly. I was the one who gave us away. Marumuk trusts him, Feelah. Completely. Thief is good at what he does."

She glanced at me. "Maybe so. But thieves are for catching, and a caught thief is a dead one."

"We will not be caught," I assured her.

"We?" Pippa turned to me.

"*He* . . . will not be caught," I said. There was no further time for talk. Already we had reached a main path leading to the back walls of the town. A trumpet blared, and I could hear many voices.

"Friends, friends!" Father cried.

The woods ended and the walls of the town appeared. Anxious faces peered down at us as we passed through the gate.

"They have come!"

"Soldiers! They bring soldiers!"

Father Bergoin stood at the center of the courtyard. Small and wizened, he leaned on his staff. His eyes, however, sparkled with the same wisdom and strength I had seen from the first. Women, farmers, children, and churchmen looked on.

Marumuk called me to him. His movements were swift and telling, as in the middle of a raid, and his hand rested firmly on his sword hilt. "Coriko, you will speak for me. Tell the churchman everything I say. And hurry. There is little time. Introduce me . . . now."

Father winked at me as I hurried toward Father Bergoin. I could hear Marumuk's heavy footfalls behind me.

"Welcome again, child." Father Bergoin nodded to me. He gazed over my shoulder. "Your mate was correct, was she not?" He smiled. The crowd pressed around us and quickly fell silent as we began to speak.

"Yes. She was." I took a deep breath. "Father Bergoin, we are in haste and need to speak quickly. This"—I stood aside—"is Marumuk, lord of the Spears and the mountain of Grassland. He comes, in our time of need, to offer assistance."

The two men stared at each other, weighing, searching. I waited for one of them to speak. A trickle of sweat worked its way down my neck. Someone squeezed my hand. Pippa was beside me. She smiled encouragingly.

I glanced from one leader to the other. "This is Marumuk," I said again, stupidly.

Bergoin cleared his throat. "The lord of Grassland is most welcome to the town of Gotten." He nodded to Marumuk.

Tia whispered softly to her husband, "It is customary to remove your helmet when speaking to churchmen." He removed his helmet.

"Churchman Bergoin," his deep voice rumbled. "We will speak in private of our plans for war. In the meantime, my men will need food and water before they are assigned positions. There is little time." He looked at the crowds around us. "And I would tell your people to go about their business. The Outside will send scouts. You can expect them at any moment. They will be watching for anything unusual. We do not want them prepared for us. Our presence must be a surprise for when the army arrives."

Father Bergoin frowned. "Joy is difficult to suppress at the best of times. Your presence, I hope, is an answer to more prayers than you can possibly imagine. I cannot wipe the smiles from their faces. I will, however," his lips twitched, "encourage the people to be more discreet."

Once again the man of war and the man of prayer stared at each other. Then they began to speak quickly, and I was kept busy relaying their words in Spear and in the Northern language.

"He knows nothing of war," Marumuk growled.

Tia stroked his arm. "And yet he wields a power, my lord."

"Yes."

"And there is little time."

Marumuk grunted.

Tia caught my eye. "Take us to where we can speak privately, Coriko. Plans must be set."

"Father—" I began.

"I know what he wants," the old man murmured. "And we will get there at my speed."

We followed Father Bergoin back to the refuge of the church and the roaring hearth fires. Churchmen moved about, their robes swishing across the stone floors. All of them smiled and nodded courteously.

"Now, this is a place of peace." Pippa's small voice echoed.

"May it always be so," Bergoin murmured. "We will go to the tower chapel. It provides the most privacy and commands an excellent view of the road."

A winding stair, with walls close on either side, took us to the top of a chamber with wood floors and several windows, one of them stained with colors. The floor swam with yellows and blues and reds in the morning sun. Father Bergoin sat at one of the two benches placed at the center of the room. He indicated for us to take the other.

Marumuk examined the room for strength, staring out the windows and testing the doors. I remained standing, as did Thief. Father sat beside the older churchman.

Father Bergoin watched the tall Spear shrewdly. "What are your intentions, Lord of Grassland, now that you are here? For surely a war leader does not easily offer his men for battle unprovoked, or without a price. Even more so when the numbers are against him. It is no small thing for our town to turn against its oppressor, especially when we are about to place our trust in so tiny an army. And one that has often enough brought raiders of its own to our shores."

The moment I gave his words to Marumuk, the soldier spun on his heels to face Bergoin. "We do not come to wage a major battle. We come with stealth. Our purpose is to take Rokhan hostage—to capture him before a single arrow is loosed—and to bring him back to the mountain where he can spend his days ensuring that his armies do not attack us."

The old man's eyebrows went up. "A hostage?"

Marumuk nodded. "A hostage, and a ruse." He paced the floor. "I will need all of your churchmen and every townsman available to stand on the walls. We have brought helmets and spears on the ships. When Rokhan looks up at these walls he must see an army that causes him to pause, to spend a night in thought before he bends his arm forward to the attack. It is in the hours of darkness that we must strike." I was working hard to explain his words and Pippa had to whisper to me twice to make the proper meaning.

"A small band will wait in the woods," he continued. "Under the cover of night, Thief will find Rokhan. Rokhan will be captured and secretly taken back to the town of Gotten. In the daylight a messenger will be sent to his commanders, with his personal belongings to be shown as proof of his capture." He waited for me to catch up. "If need be, we will dangle him from the walls in the darkness should daylight prove to be too long a wait.

149

When the Outside army has left, we will set sail again for our mountain, taking their king with us."

When Marumuk had finished, Father Bergoin tapped his lips thoughtfully. "And what is to stop the Outside army from reducing Gotten to rubble?"

Marumuk said nothing.

Tia answered. "I do not think, Father, that the Outside will attack Gotten when the alliance between the Spears and Gotten is made obvious. Outside will know that Rokhan has been brought to Grassland as the Spears' prisoner. And it is from Grassland's mountain that letters from Rokhan to his commanders will be sent, enforcing a peace."

"An alliance?" Bergoin said quietly. "Is that what we commence here, my daughter?"

Tia's eyes glistened as she turned first to me, then Pippa. "With all my heart, I pray that it is so."

Bergoin frowned. "An alliance with child stealers? Slavers?"

Tia pointed toward the window. "And what is your alliance now, Father? Money to a bloodthirsty army that kills at random and pillages where it will?"

He smiled. "Not an alliance. Only for the purpose of keeping them from spilling more blood."

"Our ways are changing, Father Bergoin," Tia countered. "Pippa and Coriko will have told you that or you would not have come to us." She looked tired and Marumuk motioned for her to sit.

The old man stared out the window. He rose slowly, gripping the back of the bench, and looked out to the road from where, soon enough, an enemy would be coming. "I did not think that when I took the spiritual leadership of this town, it would someday lead to the removal of a king." He rested his hand on the top of Feelah's head. "Or that help would come from the least expected places." He turned to Marumuk. "Do what you must to save Gotten. I ask only that you are kind to the people and that no soldier under your command extends the bounds of his duties. We will provide what food and shelter we can. I will give orders for all of the brothers to stand at the walls as you wish. God have mercy on our souls."

8

THE ARMY OF OUTSIDE CAME

before dusk the following day. The waning sun glinted off bridles and shields, and rows of spears pierced the deepening night. I did not watch from the safety of the walls of Gotten, nor did I see their numbers swell from the tower where we had set our plans. Instead, I stood close behind a tree, twenty strides from the road, hoping like the small band of Spears around me that we would not be seen.

Pippa had wept. She knew I was going with them. And I think she understood. She kissed me hard, right in front of her father.

"All that I am is with you," she said. "Know that, in your darkest moments." Then she hugged Thief.

It was difficult to recognize my friend. In Marumuk's wisdom, each of us was dressed in the ragged garb of an Outside soldier. My own breeches were tattered, and a large piece of worn tent served as a cape. The helmet did not cover my face and I felt terribly exposed. Even our swords were those from the town, instead of our own shard-made weapons. Feelah clung to Thief until Tia pulled her away.

By the time we had left the town, Spears were everywhere in Gotten. Marumuk had swelled their numbers with townspeople and brothers from the church, so that Outside would think there were many more than we actually were.

As we slipped out the rear gate and into the woods, I saw Pippa's bright hair from the walls before we disappeared into the trees.

To my surprise, Father came with us. I did not think that Marumuk would allow it, but he made no protest when the churchman joined our band.

Father winked at me. "It's best that you have someone close at hand to pray."

My heart was the better for having him with us. And

now, as the gloom deepened and the horses' breath spilled clouds into the cold air, I held to my tree as if it were Pippa.

Marumuk moved like a shadow among us.

Be strong, be silent, he signed close to our faces as he passed. Rezah was behind me. He touched my back from time to time so I would know he was still there. And somewhere in our band, Hammoth stood waiting. I wished with all my heart that he had not come, but Marumuk valued his sword.

More than any in our group, Thief waited anxiously for the darkness to settle. Our lives depended on his stealth and he knew it. He had not spoken since leaving Feelah, and did not return my encouraging smile.

"My sword will be the first to strike before a hair of your head is touched," I had whispered to him when we left the town.

Marumuk had spoken to each of us at length in the tower, and it was his courage that allowed me to be strong. "Stealth. Silence," he said. "In and out of their camp before they know we have come. We will have to speak from time to time, as this is not a normal raid. But as little as possible." He stood to his full height. "Brother for brother, sword for sword. There is strength in stone."

"And two are better than one," we finished.

We hid in the woods, where the road could still be seen and the underbrush provided enough cover when we crouched. Rokhan seemed to hold no fear of Gotten. He rode at the front of his troop wearing a helmet painted like the face of a bull. Two horns branched from either side of his head. His shield was black and painted the same as his visor. His white horse stood out from all the others and a flaming black cape flowed from his back.

Marumuk grunted.

My heart almost failed as the last horse passed along the road beside us. Two hundred soldiers. It was more than we had thought, and twice our own number. *Oh Pippa, be safe!*

Marumuk showed no concern and raised his hand. Thief rose quickly and we slipped after him like foxes to a coop.

Days of training in the Grove had taught us how to walk at night in the woods, and everything that Marumuk had shown me came back to my hands and feet. We followed along beside the army, knowing that Rokhan would allow his ragged soldiers to flow around him once the road broadened at the main gate. He did not disappoint. The rear guard broke away from the main party and rode quickly to either flank. In the center, closest to the gate, Rokhan stared up at the walls.

Father Bergoin had done all the Spears had asked, and more. Torches suddenly burst into flame, hundreds of them filling the ramparts. Everywhere the eye fell, tall forms stood waiting, watching the army below.

Rokhan's horse reared and he turned, raising his sword in the air. He roared like an animal and shook his sword at the gates. Then he pulled hard on his reins and raced back to the entrance of the road, his army swarming behind him like bees. Marumuk chuckled.

Yet even as I looked, the smile fell from my face. Around the king a tight knot of warriors gathered, raising their shields above their heads. He was well protected. It took little experience to know that he would be heavily guarded in the darkest hours of the night. Marumuk had seen it too. He found a patch of light between the trees and held his hand up so we could see.

Patience. Watch for sentries in the woods.

I shouldered my bow. Seven arrows were in my quiver. How desperately I hoped not to use any of them.

Moments later, two small groups of soldiers broke away from the main mass of the army and headed for the woods on either side of the road. So far, Marumuk had predicted the king's moves with perfect accuracy. Now the guards would be set in place, just inside the trees, while the king and his men decided what to do. Marumuk hoped that he would send a messenger to the gate, inviting surrender, and to gain some knowledge of what army had dared take the town in his absence.

But he was not a fool, this Rokhan. He wanted to be certain of his foe before he made his move.

Marumuk received his first surprise. The sentries who moved into the woods brought torches with them. They set the oil lamps ablaze some twenty strides inside the trees, then stood back closer to the road to take their posts. It was a clever trick to have sentries near the woods—yet not too near. The light would reveal any attacker who came from the trees, yet allowed the sentry to stand in the relative safety of darkness. There were five of them on our side of the woods, spaced thirty or forty strides apart.

Marumuk cursed under his breath. "Clever to force an enemy into the light. He keeps the sentry safe. Or so he thinks!" I glanced furtively at Thief. He shrugged. We waited for the army to set up its tents and start the cooking fires. Soon the woods echoed with the sound of men's voices as they gathered fuel and prepared for the long night.

My old master had been right. This ragged army liked to burn. First a band of them set ablaze all the buildings that leaned against the walls of the town. Flaming arrows breached the darkness and sank into everything made of wood. At first I thought they were trying to light the town on fire. They rode quickly toward the walls, released their arrows, then raced away, expecting an assault from above. None came. Marumuk had given strict orders that not a single arrow was to be loosed until he gave the signal.

Thief leaned against me. "They are trying to frighten the town. Rokhan wants to see who has come to fight him."

I nodded. "And he needs time to make his plans."

It was not long before the ground under the full moon was covered with tents and small fires. Wafts of smoke and warm air drifted through the trees to our chilly hiding place. My arms grew stiff with waiting. When the last glimmer of daylight had left the sky, I stirred and looked up at the sound of hoofbeats. Four horsemen were pounding their way to the town gate. They carried a flag of truce that snapped in the firelight as they rode.

Marumuk signaled to Hammoth and he quickly climbed a tree. He was gone for a long while. I flexed my fingers, waiting.

"They are returning!" Hammoth whispered suddenly. The thud of hooves made me strain to see through the gaps in the trees to the torchlight. We waited anxiously for Hammoth's report.

A hand touched my shoulder. Father.

"How do you fare, lad?"

"All is well." Father's white-flecked hair stood out silver in the torchlight from the nearest sentry's post. He looked calm, yet alert. "Do you have a weapon?" I asked. He shook his head. I pulled out my dagger and held it out to him.

He smiled and gently brushed it aside. "I cannot do that, lad. It wouldn't be right to kill when I am meant to save. No, I'll knock heads if I have to. But no blades."

I smiled weakly. I would have to watch over him. A man without a weapon in these woods was as good as dead. Even Pippa could want no less.

A slight scrabbling noise from the tree made our heads turn. Hammoth was reporting back to Marumuk.

"They spoke for a while at the gate," he whispered. "The old churchman did most of the talking, from what I could see. The messengers were angry when they left."

Marumuk grunted. "Good. What of the tower?"

Hammoth nodded. "The torches went out briefly. Then came on again. Outside also cut down trees on the other side of the road."

Marumuk smiled grimly. "The signal! Bergoin was to show it if Rokhan gave him some time to consider surrender. This means that they have given us until morning to make a decision. In the meantime, Rokhan prepares ladders for scaling the walls at dawn. If they are lying about their intentions and attack immediately, we will return to the town. For now, we wait."

"What of the sentries near the woods?" Rezah asked. "We had not counted on those."

"I will show you what to do when the time comes," Marumuk answered. He looked at me. "Keep your fingers warm. I will need your bow before the night is over. Be swift, little brothers. And do not hold back."

Outside did not attack. They were allowing Gotten until morning to make their decision. I kept my hands inside my ragged cloak and cursed the cold air. Father's large frame blocked the breeze from the sea, for which I thanked him silently. The Outside soldiers, weary from several days' journey, maintained a painstaking watchfulness. The night was thick with a brooding malice.

Sometime later Marumuk stood. He rose slowly in the dim light, keeping his eyes on the nearest sentry. He moved toward me, beckoning also to Thief and the others.

"This is the hour. We will enter the camp from here." Marumuk glanced at me and nodded toward the guard. "He must fall to the ground without noise. Hit his throat."

Beside me, Father groaned.

"Walk into the camp as if you were Outside soldiers,"

Marumuk went on. "Walk with purpose, but if anyone comes too near, make it seem as if you are heavy with sleep."

To the others he said, "Follow Thief and Coriko in pairs, at a distance. Rezah and I will be with them. Do not come near Rokhan. If we are found out, come to our aid quickly, for there is more hope of us leaving this sleeping camp alive than fighting an awakened army in the morning." Without a further word, he gave me the signal. Pulling my hands out from my cloak, I began to work my fingers, tightening and relaxing them. I unslung my bow and pulled an arrow from the quiver. Father made to speak, but Marumuk held him back.

With all my heart and with all the strength in my hands . . . I stared at the burning torches where Pippa watched from the walls. A little house . . . our own place of peace . . . my beautiful Pippa. *Perhaps I could hit his helmet.* On the ship, on the way back to Gotten, Pippa said she wanted to have children one day. I did not know what to say. She had burst into giggles. *His chest. If I loosed the arrow properly, it might take his wind and drop him without penetrating his armor.* A house . . . freedom . . . a family . . .

I glanced at Father. He was sweating. Somehow I knew it was not from fear. I searched his face. There was no judgment. Only grief.

The sentry raised his chin to scratch at his scruffy beard. His entire throat lay open to me.

I will try, Pippa. I will try.

I fired. The arrow nicked the sentry's helmet and shot off into the woods. Marumuk started to run toward him from the bushes.

Peace. Calm.

Stunned, the guard stumbled into the torchlight toward us. I loosed my second arrow.

The tip struck the sentry's helmet with such force his forehead rocked backward. His eyes rolled back. Marumuk caught him before he struck the ground, and dragged him to thicker woods and waning torchlight. Hammoth and Rezah pulled the sentry into the curtain of leaves.

Smile, Pippa, I thought. *That was close.*

Marumuk stood up. Then he walked back into the light of the torch and took the sentry's pose, guarding the woods as if nothing had happened. I fitted another arrow and scanned the woods. There was no sound of alarm.

Marumuk finally signaled us forward. Only Father remained behind.

"You do not look like a soldier," I whispered to him. "You look like a churchman."

He grinned back at me. "Go with God, Son. My prayers are with you."

Thief's breath came in little wheezes. We crept on all fours until we passed Marumuk. Heartbeats later he joined us, and I turned to see Hammoth standing in his place by the torch.

At least he is not coming with us into the camp, I thought.

We stood slowly as the woods ended and the mouth of the road opened. We were walking among the tents of Outside. Marumuk no longer moved with stealth. He drooped his great shoulders and eased his stride. My own legs shook with each step.

Thief had found his strength again. Gripping my hand, he pulled us away from the others. He moved quickly, confidently, and seemed to know his way around the tents as if he had been in Rokhan's pay all his life. I risked a look over my shoulder and caught sight of Marumuk and Rezah following at a distance.

Everywhere I looked, steaming pots hung over small fires, and the odor of a pungent stew lay thick on the night air. The smell of sweaty leather and horse dung was a nauseating reminder that Gotten was coming under siege by a large army. Equipment was sprawled outside each tent, making walking as hazardous as crossing a river over wet stones. Here and there we caught a glimpse of guards. I stiffened every time they came near. Thief led us steadily to the center of the camp, picking his way expertly through the maze of sleeping soldiers. I clung to his shadow as if he held my life in his hand. And he did.

He stopped. I did not need him to point. The king had a cluster of men around his tent. They formed a rough circle of sleeping forms, their weapons resting beside their heads or backs. *No shelter for these ones*, I thought. Nor did they look as if they needed any. These were the toughest looking warriors I had ever seen. They were huge, every one of them, and their weapons were unusually large. They slept with the confidence of a battle already won. Three of them were close enough for us to see their faces. Each one had a blue tattoo etched across the side of his cheek. I could not make out what the picture was, but it looked frightening enough from a distance. I had no wish to look closer.

I bit my lip. We were ruined. There was no possible way of getting at Rokhan.

But I had forgotten our thief. He put his mouth to my ear. "Watch this."

With eyes shining, he did the most unexpected thing I could have imagined.

Striding up as if to pass the circle of sleeping guards, he paused and stretched. A soldier walked past us, heading for the far side of the camp. He did not even look at us. I eased my dagger back into its sheath.

Thief yawned loudly. He finished his stretch, then lay down between the closest guards, looking like a minnow among whales. My mouth fell open. I waited for the men to kill him. The soldier to his left began to stir. Thief sensed his movement and, raising his feet, kicked the man's legs. The guard cursed but did not turn fully over. Thief fought for more space between the two guards until he won it with elbows or kicks. I sank to the ground in disbelief.

Marumuk and Rezah passed by the circle, walking drunkenly. Thief's head lifted and stared back at me. He grinned.

I groaned. Idiot! Clever little idiot!

He lay still for a while and I tried to keep my own head from jerking around at every snore or crackle from the fires. Sometime later Thief moved again. He turned slowly until he lay on his stomach. Raising himself onto his knees, he inched his way toward the tent, stopping once in a while to wait. His dagger suddenly flashed from his belt. The flap of Rokhan's tent fluttered in the night air. I could not look. I searched for Marumuk and Rezah, only to watch them frozen, staring at Thief. When I turned back to the tent, he was gone and the entrance flap hung open.

There was a silence so deadly I wanted to shout. I wanted daylight to pierce the darkness and give me back my friend. A murmur came from inside the tent, followed by an intake of breath.

I knelt in the shadow of the nearest tent, my bow off my shoulder and pulled tight, an arrow aimed at the king's shelter. The flap stirred. My heart sank at the sight of Rokhan's shaggy head pushing through the opening with his braids flailing. He was enormous. But right behind him, with a dagger at the back of Rokhan's neck, came Thief. I aimed for the king's head. He saw me and glared

167

with murderous eyes. His gaze flickered to his guards, but he did not make a sound. There was a trickle of blood dripping from the front of his throat.

I almost screamed when a voice called out a question to the king. I could not see who had called out, but someone was sitting up. It was not one of the guards within my direct sight. I could make out a leg and arm. Thief's knife dug a little deeper. It was clear, to Rokhan at least, that my friend was quite capable of ending his life before his men could reach him. A dead king could not win a battle.

Rokhan mumbled something back and the soldier lay down. With the knife's prompting, the king walked through the space that Thief had made between the guards.

The moment he was out past the guards, Marumuk appeared. He slipped behind Rokhan and took over Thief's grip. The king must have felt the difference immediately, for his face changed and he did not try to look around to see who held him. Marumuk nodded for us to leave. We moved swiftly, choosing the fastest route to the woods. Thief led us through the maze of tents. His arm shook and I squeezed his fingers. Partway back to the woods I took over the lead, slowing our pace and moving with more caution. I looked back incessantly at Marumuk. He brought the king along steadily, twenty strides behind. Rezah was somewhere behind them.

At the sight of Hammoth, relief caught up with me at last. The torchlight was brighter here and Hammoth turned quickly at the sound of our footsteps. It must have been difficult for him to be standing on his own, waiting for us, fearing to be discovered.

Peace, I signed.

Wild excitement filled my heart. We had the king! *Pippa, we are coming!*

As we approached, I felt forgiveness wash over me. I would have hugged Hammoth if danger were not so close at hand. But he turned away as if he had not heard us.

"Hammoth!" I whispered. I stumbled in the sudden light of the torches, and Thief leaped ahead to steady me. When Hammoth swung around again he raised his weapon.

"Hammoth!"

Without a word, the Spear plunged his dagger into Thief.

9

H

HAMMOTH SNARLED AND pulled his dagger free. He came at me. My shock was so great I hardly had time to raise my own blade. Beside me, Thief slumped and fell. Blinding wrath flowed through my veins. With my free hand I punched Hammoth in the head and he went down. He rolled as he touched the ground, then leapt to his feet to avoid my death stroke.

Voices erupted behind us and as I charged forward, swinging and cutting with a fury, the sound of the other sentries' heavy footfalls echoed in the woods.

"Coriko," Thief gasped.

Spinning away from the fleeing Hammoth, I returned to my friend. He was on his knees, his hands full of blood clasped at his chest. I held him around the waist and raised him to his feet. Marumuk strode up with Rokhan firmly in his grasp.

"Run!" he grunted. He stared in confusion, looking from me to Thief. Rokhan lurched to get away and Marumuk gripped his wild hair like reins. "Run, Coriko!"

Flinging away my bow, I hoisted Thief onto my shoulder. From the corner of my eye I saw Rezah swing his sword at the standing torch. The forest was instantly plunged into darkness. My burden eased a moment later and I realized that Rezah was taking some of Thief's weight. We crashed through the woods with Outside guards shouting behind us. An arrow whistled past my head and sank into a tree. Another ripped some bark from a trunk, viciously spraying my face. My eyes adjusted to the dark and I concentrated on the forest floor, trying to avoid roots and fallen logs. Thief groaned with every step until he finally fell silent and limp. Tears poured from my face.

"Give him to me, lad!" Father suddenly said beside me. His robes were tied up at his belt as he ran with the rest of us. He rolled Thief from my shoulder. "Follow Marumuk," he ordered. "I'm right behind you."

Blood covered my arms. Thief's warm blood. I ran after Marumuk and the king. More arrows whizzed around us. In the madness of our flight to the town I had a sudden moment of clarity and realized that Hammoth was running beside me. He looked at me.

"I didn't know it was Thief!" he gasped when our shoulders touched. "I didn't know. I swear, I thought you were Rokhan's men."

I pushed him off.

"I will *kill* you, Hammoth."

"Be silent!" came Rezah's warning. "They will come quickly now, on foot, through the trees. They must not be allowed to follow our voices."

And then we heard the cry. The king's absence had been noticed. The entire camp was astir, men shouting and horses whinnying. The missing sentry had been noticed at last. We could see the Outside soldiers' torches, at least fifty, gleaming, as the soldiers clustered at the road closest to the forest's edge. A moment later they plunged like a flaming wave into the trees after us.

But there was still another terror.

"Marumuk!" Rezah hissed. "They are coming for us.

And more are attacking the town on horseback!" A line of torches bobbed wildly along the road as the soldiers rode toward the front gates. Horses neighed and stamped, somewhere close by.

"Faster!" the big Spear grunted. "We must get to the rear gate before they surround the town. They will try to keep us from reaching it." He did not need to encourage me. My blade was out and I raced ahead of him. More than anything, Thief needed to be brought behind the walls. It was the last thing I could do for him and with all my heart I swore that I would. I did not care about the king anymore. I could only think of making the way clear so that my friend could get to safety. Branches slapped my cheeks and several times I sprawled, once letting go of my sword.

The soldiers behind us were spreading out, searching behind every tree. Breaking through the last of the woods, I listened and searched the darkness of the harbor. No lights, other than those shining from the walls, would reveal us to enemy eyes. The Outside army had not yet circled Gotten's walls and already I could hear them pounding against the front gates.

"Get the gates open!" Marumuk called.

I could hear him wrestling with Rokhan. Racing shadows appeared ahead, made grotesquely large by the torchlight.

"They are coming!" I shouted. No sooner had the words left my mouth than arrows began to cut through the air.

"The gates!" Marumuk yelled.

I ran the short distance to the gates, ducking and leaping, waiting for the jarring pain of an arrow in my side.

I passed into the safety of the wall's shadow and pounded on the metal gates as hard as I could. "Open!" I cried. "Marumuk comes with a gift! Open, open, open!"

I slammed the gates with my sword, then turned back to watch the shadowy forms of my laboring friends as they stumbled across the short grass. I leaned against the stone wall and peered around the corner. Soldiers were swarming toward us. Torches were being hurled from the parapet and archers fired down into the swelling crowd of Outsiders.

"Open!" someone finally called above me. With a grinding creak the gates swung wide. Five Spears pushed me aside and ran out onto the field, shields raised. They formed a knot around Marumuk. Rokhan no longer resisted and it was clear that Marumuk had knocked the man senseless.

One of the Spears took Thief from Father. The churchman was puffing hard but managed to keep up the last few steps.

Screams erupted from the courtyard.

"Mercy," Father gasped, bending to catch his breath. Two large Spears heaved the gates closed and a bar was set in place to lock them. We faced the madness within.

Arrows poured over the tops of the battlements and landed in the courtyard like hail, slashing and clattering against the stones. Everywhere I looked, people were pressed against the walls or hiding behind barrels. Others ran for open doorways. Still others made desperate lunges to get to the shelter of the stone church. Three bodies lay sprawled on the stones, and I stared with grim understanding at the feathers sticking up from the still forms. Several of the merchants' carts had caught fire and a pot of scattered coals glowed ominously from the flagstones.

All of us paused, waiting for a break in the arrows to run for the church. I put my hand on Thief's arm. His skin was cold.

"Thief, Thief!" I cried.

"Marumuk!" a soldier screamed. "They are scaling the wall!"

"Take Rokhan within!" the big Spear commanded. He shoved the unconscious king into waiting hands. Hurling off his Outside cloak, he quickly donned his own helmet and cape. Our own clothing hung behind us on pegs and I hastily followed Marumuk. Beside my now empty peg, Thief's cape stared back at me. I buckled on his sword and kept my own, free of its scabbard, in one hand.

"Take Rokhan to the top tower," Marumuk yelled to a Spear Master. "Wake him up! Be ready to thrust his face over the parapet at my order. I want his army to see that we have him alive. Get the men off the forward wall. Archers only will stay. I want battle lines at the gates in case they breach. Take Thief to the churchmen."

Marumuk faced us—a small band of Spears, and the only ones I could see who were not hurrying into battle position.

My friend was gone. I would have followed him had Marumuk not stopped me. His eyes caught each of us and held us fast. Beyond the walls we could hear the howls of men's anger, the agony of the wounded, and the pounding of wood as the Outside attacked the gates with new fury.

"We will take the forward wall. Do not let any who scale the top live. Most of all, do not let them near the tower where Rokhan is held, or all is lost. Be brave tonight, my brothers!" To my surprise, he reached out and gripped my shoulder. "I need your sword, Coriko. Fight beside me. Think of nothing else until the dawn!" He squeezed hard. "Fight until the dawn."

"Yes, my lord." The words came out. In that place and in that moment Marumuk was still my master.

He saluted. "Follow my lead in everything. The night is ours, for we have the king!" He raised his sword high. "There is strength in stone . . ."

Around me the voices of Spears took up the chant. "And two are better than one!"

"We fight!" Marumuk yelled. "Do you hear me? *We fight!*"

"We fight!" we all echoed. I charged forward with the others, no less than three strides behind Marumuk, across the arrow-ridden courtyard to the stone stairs that led to the battlements. I set my eyes on Marumuk's cape, and for a moment I was back in the Grove. All else disappeared, and sword and flesh and blood were all that I could feel.

The Outside had scaled the walls. Although they had time to construct only crude ladders, the moment I reached the top of the battlements, a blade came slashing for my head. I blocked and pulled him past me. The man's yell stopped short when he hit the courtyard below.

No sooner had I recovered when a second blade lunged for my chest. I countered and slashed back, feeling the tip of my sword strike hard against his wooden shield, the vibration from the blow shivering up my arms. Arrows sped past our heads, whistling toward their targets. My opponent was an experienced fighter. He was large, and as he leaned forward to return the blow, I saw him clearly. A dark tattoo—a grinning bull—covered half his face. My sword shattered as our weapons came together.

I stumbled. Searing pain shot through my elbow. As my enemy stepped over me to finish his work, I saw a wooden staff whistle past. It crashed down on the Outsider's wrist and with a howl of pain he dropped his weapon.

Father stepped forward, his staff again at the ready. He stared evenly at the soldier and squared his feet. "Run,

Outsider. Or I shall have to use this on your head."

The guard roared and swung a mighty fist at the churchman. Father nimbly stepped back, then struck out with his staff again, cracking it against the side of the guard's face.

"Mercy! That must have hurt," Father said. "Learn from the pain, my son. My staff is most unforgiving."

I regained my feet. Thief's sword shone in the darkness, its pommel comforting in my hand.

The Outsider shook his head and ripped a dagger from his belt, bellowing like a bull.

"Folly in the face of mercy!" Father shouted. "Take warning, my son, for my staff is coming for you!" Before I could swing my blade, Father feinted to one side. The guard followed his movement and raised his shield. Stepping to his open side, Father brought his staff down with a fury. The king's guard landed on his back and did not move.

"Take care, child," Father called to me. Then he raced into the swirling bodies fighting on the parapet with his cloak billowing like a storm cloud.

"Rezah! Coriko!" Marumuk desperately tried to push a ladder back from the wall. An Outsider, clinging to the top rung, swung viciously at Marumuk's helmet. We raced to his side. I took the man on the ladder while Rezah protected us from the fighting on the parapet. The soldier cut and jabbed. After each strike at me he would swing at Marumuk.

Marumuk ducked. "Get him now!"

I grasped the sword with both hands and delivered the hardest blow I could muster. Although it landed against the man's sword, he teetered back, momentarily letting go of the ladder. Marumuk reached forward and pushed him hard in the chest. The soldier fell off with a short wheeze.

"Push it over!" Marumuk roared.

We stood shoulder to shoulder and heaved on the wooden frame. My arm still ached from the blow the guard had given me, but I pushed with all my strength. The ladder hardly moved. Another pair of hands joined ours. From the corners of my eyes I recognized him. Hammoth. The ladder moved, slowly, agonizingly slowly. More Outsiders leaped onto the ladder, but we had tipped the balance. The frame moved from the wall. The top man scrambled to reach us. The ladder fell backward at a sickening rate, flinging its occupants off like ants.

We leaned on our knees, gasping for air, and stared along

the parapet. Sweat dripped from my chin, splashing to the stones. There were four Outsiders still in sight. Two of them were busy slashing at the tower door. The other two were coming right for us. There were bulls tattooed on their faces.

Marumuk pointed to the tower. "Now is the time! Hammoth, with me. We take the first two. Rezah, Coriko, get to the tower. There is a flag of truce inside. You must bring it out. The night hangs in the balance. Do not fail!"

The bull warriors charged. Marumuk and Hammoth met them only a few strides from us and four blades clashed. I ducked through an opening of arms and legs, and squirmed past them. Rezah's pounding feet sounded after me. We raced along the parapet, keeping our heads low to avoid arrows. We rushed past Father, who knelt beside the wounded. We raced past the bodies of churchmen, stuck with arrows, their peaceful prayers now silent. One of the soldiers battering the door saw us coming and swung around. Rezah threw his dagger and the man fell before we reached him.

The remaining soldier turned from the door and lifted his axe. From the size of it, I was amazed that the door had not burst open already. He swung. It took both our swords to keep from being flattened. Hardly had he finished his first swipe when he kicked my legs out from under me. I knew his downward swing was coming and rolled away. He kicked me again and my body slid toward the edge of the parapet, like a wet fish thrown across smooth stone. Suddenly I was staring into the courtyard far below. There were more bodies there now. It was a long way down and the stones at the bottom were unforgiving. "Pippa!" I gasped. "I won't leave you!"

I gripped Thief's sword and rolled, finding further room on the parapet. Although my chest was heaving with exhaustion, a new rage swept through me. Rezah and the soldier had just locked weapons. My shoulder caught the man off balance and he staggered backward, slamming into the tower door. I fell on my backside, staring up at him. Before he could raise his axe again, his mouth opened in surprise. No sound came out. Instead, his eyes rolled back in his head and he fell, like a hewn tree, on top of me.

"Get him off!" I wheezed.

Rezah helped me turn him, and the man's body flopped over. Sticking out from the barred grate in the door, a spear tip suddenly pulled back into the darkness of the tower.

Rezah lifted me to my feet.

"Open!" I cried. "It is Coriko! It is Coriko!"

A face appeared between the bars. Metal screeched along locking rails. Warm air rushed out as the door opened and we were suddenly staring at gaping faces. The stillness inside was shocking after the chaos outside. Five or six Spears stood at the back wall, swords at the ready. Rokhan sat on the floor with a sack over his head. There were others as well, but my eyes could not adjust so quickly.

"Corki!" Pippa stepped into the torchlight. "You're covered in blood . . . "

"My child?" That was Bergoin.

I wanted to run to Pippa. I wanted to find Thief. I wanted to get away from the tower, from the king, from this cold land. Tia was in front of me. In one hand she held a spear, its tip bloodied. In the other, she clutched a white cloth. Her face was tight with worry and the spear shook in her hands. Yet, as always, she showed the strength of a queen.

"My brave Coriko."

"It is bad, Tia." My voice cracked. "Thief—"

"I know." Those keen eyes that had led us out of Grassland gave me the strength I needed. She thrust the cloth into my bloodied fingers. "Finish the night, my brave boy. For all of us."

I nodded. Pippa's face was white and her eyes shifted to another figure beside her.

Feelah.

I could not speak.

"Where is my Thief?" she whispered. For the first time I noticed Bran, holding tightly to her shoulders. All those I loved in one place together. Almost all of them.

"I'll be back," I croaked. "I have to . . . this flag . . . I'll be back." But I did not want to. I did not want to see Feelah's pain ever again.

"Coriko!" Rezah called. "They are sending up another ladder."

I backed out of the room and Rezah heaved the door closed. My breath came in gasps. Hammoth stood on the parapet beside Marumuk, glancing to me, then back over the wall at the Outside army, as any good Spear would do. *As if nothing had happened in the woods.*

In my hands I held a flag of truce, the hope of all we had planned for. In the other, a sword belonging to my dearest friend, cut down by a traitor. A traitor! I could not shake the image of Feelah's face, hopeless, pain filled.

"Coriko?" Another ladder clattered into position against the wall, and Marumuk turned from me.

I hefted the sword. *One quick thrust and it would be over for Hammoth.*

Marumuk called again, urgently.

One quick thrust.

"Coriko! Hold the flag over the side. Do it. Now!"

I unfurled the cloth and thrust it over the side, keeping myself tucked low to the wall. Arrows whined around me, several striking the wall so close to the flag that splinters of stone bounced off the back of my hand.

Marumuk shouted orders to the Spear archers in the lower courtyard to cease fire.

Rezah knelt beside me, his chest spattered with blood. "What happened to Thief?"

Our eyes met. "Hammoth."

And then the battle stopped. Only the shouting continued: from the ground, from the courtyard, and from the walls. The harsh tongue of the Outsiders, the language of Gotten, and the speech of Grassland clashed together in the night air. After a while Marumuk stood up plainly and looked down. No arrows were fired.

"Bring out the king!" he called to me.

I rose from my crouch. Picking up the axe from the fallen Outsider, I hooked an edge of the flag of truce underneath it so that it could hang clearly from the wall. The army of Outside stood below; a hundred bows aimed at my head. My feet were frozen. My sword called for Hammoth.

Father stared at me questioningly.

"Coriko." Rezah tugged at me. "Come, friend. Together we will get the king."

My lips quivered with fury. "Hammoth killed Thief. He killed him. He killed my best friend."

Rezah put his helmet against my own. "There will be a time and place to set things right," he whispered. "I swear it. Even with my own hands, I will do it."

"*Now* is the time, Rezah. Now is the place."

His grip tightened. "Many lives hang in the balance this night, Coriko. Even Pippa's. Tia's life. Feelah's life. Will she join her mate in darkness before the dawn because Coriko wanted a fool's blood?"

From the courtyard I could hear a woman weeping. I let Rezah turn me. Together we walked to the door.

10

THE ROOM WAS AS STILL AS I HAD left it. Tia swung the door wide. Without looking at Pippa or Feelah, I beckoned to the guards. "Bring him," I croaked.

The Spears raised Rokhan roughly to his feet. He still had plenty of strength left in him, for he immediately began to struggle. There was little mercy. One of the Spears tightened the sack on his head so that it cut off his air. He stopped struggling.

Pippa looked at me.

I shrugged. "He needs to behave."

"Take him," Tia ordered.

"Stay in here, Pippa," I said. "Do not come out."

"She will not go out," Tia answered. And I knew from Tia's face that Pippa would not, until it was safe.

I pulled Rokhan forward.

Marumuk stood by the flag of truce, impatiently sliding his sword up and down in its sheath. Hammoth glared at Rokhan and did not look at me.

A little push and Hammoth would be with the Outside.

Marumuk took the king roughly in his grasp. "Call the churchman," he said to me, then, "we will need to use their language."

I called Father over. "Can you speak the Outside language, Father?" I asked him.

He nodded. "Most of us can."

"He can," I said aloud.

Marumuk grunted. Then he raised a hand into the air above the Outside army. A hush fell on the soldiers below. Torches sputtered and horses stamped. Father moved beside Marumuk. "We have your king!" the Spear shouted with a mighty voice.

Although he translated the words as loudly as he could, Father's voice strained in the night air compared to Marumuk's. I repeated Father's words, speaking for both of them, hardly aware of what I was saying. Marumuk leaned the king over the edge of the wall so that his head, still covered by the sack, would look out to the road below. There was a rush of voices when the Outsiders saw him. It was followed by gasps when Marumuk ripped the cover off the king's head. The wild braids came free and immediately Rokhan began to shout down to his troops.

One of the Spears stepped forward, but Marumuk held him back. "Let him speak. If he tells them to attack, then I will throw him over the edge and we will see if the god can fly! They can pick up his pieces."

Marumuk let Rokhan go on shouting, holding him by the back of his war cloak like a horse on a tether.

"What is he saying?" Marumuk asked.

Father cleared his throat. "He is describing your mother."

Marumuk laughed. "I do not remember her. But I doubt his descriptions are just."

Father winced when I gave him the words. "I hope not."

Changing his grip, Marumuk took the king by the hair. "Leave!" he shouted to the soldiers below. "All of you. Get on your horses and go. Leave your tents, leave your fires, and go. If even one of you is standing here by the dawn, I will send your king's hands to you in a bag."

There was an angry shout from below.

Marumuk raised his sword. Rokhan roared again at his men.

"He is telling them to kill everyone in the town. He tells them to hunt your children down to the next ten generations." Father paused. "He is expecting you to kill him now. He just ordered someone below to build a battering ram."

"Then tell them this," the Spear answered. "Your king will send word to you from a faraway place. If you want your god to stay alive, then leave before my mind changes. When the time is right, he will be returned to you. You have the word of Marumuk."

One of the king's guards stood and shouted at Marumuk.

Father mopped his brow with the edge of his cloak. "He says that he will have your head on a stick."

When I spoke the words, Marumuk pressed his sword against the king's neck. From the soldiers below we could hear an intake of breath.

"Caution, my son," Father whispered.

Giving his sword to me, Marumuk pulled his knife from his belt. With a quick swipe he severed a lock of the king's braid. The thick black strands waved in the breeze.

"Remember your king!" Marumuk shouted. He dropped the braid.

It landed at the feet of the king's guard.

I squeezed my eyes shut. Everything depended on what the man would do now. *Pray, Pippa, pray!*

The guard stooped to lift the braid from the ground. Rokhan's other guards pressed close around him, speaking urgently for several moments amid the groaning of the wounded. Then the guard called up to us.

Father looked at Marumuk. "He says you have chosen to battle the gods, and that the gods will have their justice with you. The army will leave now. If your word is not true, they will hunt you to the ends of the sea."

The man turned and made for the road. The Outsiders retreated from the walls. Their numbers swelled the road, their torches blazing like a fiery snake. Those who had fallen were left behind, and lay in gruesome shadows on the ground. With cursing and raised fists the soldiers rode off into the night, a dust cloud rising high into the air behind them. I clutched the stone wall in exhaustion.

"Coriko."

Pippa stood beside me, her tears caught in the torchlight. She slipped her arms around me.

Rokhan was hauled away in the company of Spears. Tia stood with Marumuk. He nodded to me. "Well done, Coriko."

"Come." Pippa tugged at me. "There is someone you must see."

"Be cautious!" Tia called after us. "Even now, with the battle won."

As we left the wall, Rezah stopped us. "I will stay with Hammoth. I will follow him wherever he goes, as long as my duties allow."

I nodded gratefully.

"Come," Pippa whispered, leading me into the church. Thief was lying there on a bed of grass, stained red in patches from his blood. Feelah knelt on the stone floor, holding his hand. Thief's face was white. It should not have been white. I stopped walking.

A churchman walked past us carrying a steaming bowl and placed it beside the bed. An older man stooped at the bedside, praying. It was Father Bergoin. He turned as we approached.

"A difficult night." He smiled sympathetically. "For all of us." I followed his gaze to a number of bodies lying on pallets near the fire.

The other churchman rose. "Apply the ointment slowly after you have cleaned the wound again with hot water," he was saying to Feelah.

"He lives?" I stammered. "Thief is *alive*?"

Feelah patted his hand. "Yes. But he has not wakened since you brought him here."

"There will be a fever soon," Father Bergoin murmured. "If he can win the morning, he may yet live to steal another king. God knows, the boy has earned it." He moved on to the next bed.

I knelt beside Thief and took his other hand. It was so cold. His eyes were moving under the lids. I waited for the confident smile to appear, but he slept on. Bran wiped Thief's face with a cloth.

"He saved us tonight," I whispered.

Pippa leaned forward and touched Thief's forehead. "Sleep for a while. Sleep well, and wake to greet us."

"And in good health!" Father chimed in. His robe was torn, and blood spattered his chest and hood. "Daughter." He received Pippa's embrace, then looked at me. "My son. This has been a night of both evil and brave deeds."

"It was Hammoth! With my own eyes I saw him thrust the knife . . ." I stopped when Feelah peered up at me.

"Treacherous!" Father rumbled.

"He says that he did not know it was us," I continued. "But he *did*!"

"Are you sure?" Pippa asked.

"Yes. It must be so. I saw him."

"Does Marumuk know?"

"No. There was no time. None at all. We ran to get here and hardly made it before the fighting started."

"What do we do?" Pippa looked at her father.

He reached out with a weathered hand and placed it on Thief's head. "You must tell Marumuk." He squinted and looked closely at me. "It seems to me that the knife could have just as likely been meant for you. Do not sleep too heavily tonight. There is treachery in the air. I will ask the brothers to watch." He straightened. "Glory! Why must there always be a thorn when the rose is just blooming?" He hurried after Father Bergoin. I looked the other way, through the tall arches of the church and to the open courtyard where Spears hurried and voices shouted.

"Your hands are trembling," Pippa said.

I looked down at my bloodstained clothes. "I have to . . . I have to . . ."

"You have to tell Marumuk," she answered for me. "That is what you have to do." When I turned to go she pulled me back. "Remember, Corki, just go and tell Marumuk. Let him be the judge."

"But Hammoth—"

"What good will revenge do? Thief is alive."

Before I could answer, a tall Spear came through the archway and strode up to us. "Coriko, my lord Marumuk would meet with you in the tower. The lady requests her friends as well." His eyes flickered over Pippa and Feelah.

"I will not go," Feelah answered.

"Nor will I." Father knelt beside Thief.

"You at least should come," I said to Bran.

With a last look at Thief and a nod at Feelah, we followed the Spear. Pippa gasped at the carnage in the courtyard. She broke into tears as bodies were lifted from the stones and taken away.

"Do not look, Pippa." I put my arm around her shoulders as we walked.

She pulled away. "I *will* look. I must." She stood silently as a churchman was lifted onto a stretcher and carried by two other brothers. He looked old. Likely he had been caught by arrows while trying to get to the safety of the church.

Pippa touched the crumpled cloak of the dead man as they passed. "He was alive yesterday," she said to me. "He was praying in the church."

"Marumuk is waiting," I murmured. We passed Rokhan being taken to the back gate. It looked as if Marumuk was wasting no time packing the king of Outside onto a ship and sending him back to Grassland.

When we reached the tower room it had been relit with candles. Tia embraced both of us. "Where is Feelah? And what news of Thief?"

My eyes shot past her to Marumuk, to Rezah, and to Hammoth, who stood cloaked in the shadow of the wall.

Spears were gathered around Marumuk as he gave new orders.

"Thief lives. Barely. The churchmen believe he will make it through the night."

Tia sighed heavily. "Feelah is with him?"

Pippa nodded. "And my father."

I took another step forward. "I need to speak with Marumuk."

"Coriko?" Tia said.

I lifted my hand to her and she took it. "I need to speak to Marumuk, Tia."

She nodded slowly.

Hammoth moved away from the wall. His gaze shifted uneasily from me to Pippa. His hand rested on his sword.

"Marumuk will speak with you soon," Tia was saying. "We are preparing to leave. And with Rokhan in our care, we cannot take any chances. Marumuk fears that Outside scouts will discover the boats in the harbor. We must be gone before full light."

"So quickly?" Pippa asked.

"We must get Rokhan to Grassland quickly. I trust that, in time, there will be many comings and goings between our two lands," Tia answered. "But let us secure the peace first. Then we may speak of happy times to come."

The talking was over. Four tall Spears strode past us, with Marumuk following closely behind.

"Marumuk—" Tia began.

"I will return shortly," he said. "There is movement in the woods, close to the boats. I want to make certain there are no Outsiders hiding among the trees."

He turned to me. "I can spare only a dozen Red Fists, Coriko. But I ask you to prepare a defense for the town should the Outside return. I do not think it will happen, but I have learned that chance is greatest when least expected. Will you keep the town?"

Hammoth's name froze on my lips. Doubt clouded my thoughts. Was it possible Hammoth did not know what he was doing?

"Most of all," he continued, "I ask you to watch over Tia."

Marumuk's concerns were with the town and winning peace—everything we had risked our lives for. The issue of Hammoth would have to wait. What mattered most was the safety of the town—and everyone in it.

"I will," I answered, bowing.

He saluted and strode out with Hammoth at his heels. My enemy did not look at me in passing. Instead his eyes slid to Pippa before he disappeared out the door. My doubt was gone.

"Put that *down.*" Pippa's voice shook.

My dagger had somehow found its way into my hands. I stared at the cracked and drying blood on my wrists, still there from the night's fighting.

Tia walked to the door and closed it. "What was that about?"

"Hammoth stabbed Thief tonight. I saw him do it."

"Hammoth!" Her face blanched. "Yes." She gazed out the window, fear suddenly filling her face. "I have always doubted his loyalty. His hunger for power is so clear to me. But not to Marumuk. Marumuk believes he is a soldier who follows orders." Then, "Did you *tell* Marumuk?"

"There was no time. Rezah vows he will be watching Hammoth."

"We must all be watchful." Tia turned to us. "I feared this. Everything we could have hoped for has happened, and yet the poison has still found its way into our midst." She reached for a bench and sat down. "Is Hammoth *part* of the rebellion, or does he *lead* it?"

"Courage, Tia." I thought of the Spears who had left with Marumuk. "There are many Masters who stand by Marumuk. He is not alone."

Pippa knelt in front of Tia. Then she suddenly placed her hands on Tia's stomach. "How much longer?" Pippa whispered.

A tear splashed on Tia's knee. "Not too much . . . Perhaps I should not have come."

Pippa touched Tia's lips. "Marumuk has the courage of a hundred," she said. "He can wave his sword around magnificently. But without his wife his mountain would crumble, and his sword would fall. In my heart, I believe that you have been given the task of turning the Spears, changing them from what they were into something that they *can* be—for you, and your child to come. This task is almost as large as asking the ocean to leave its borders."

"Yes," Tia murmured.

"I will come back with you this time," Bran whispered to her.

Pippa squeezed Tia's hands. "This task would not have been given to you if it was too great for you to accomplish."

Tia wiped a tear away. "I miss you so much," she whispered. She ran her fingers through Pippa's hair. She placed her forehead against Bran's and rested a moment. Then she stood, squared her shoulders, and turned to me. "Coriko. We must set watches at every corner of the city. We need churchmen walking the walls with lighted torches until the daylight sets in. You and Bran and Rezah must be my eyes and ears. For now I walk among some who cannot be trusted." She turned to leave, then paused. "Forgive me, Coriko. I am used to giving orders these days, and I forgot your position. I will follow you."

With a brief glance at Pippa, I drew Thief's sword. "I am on duty," I growled before she could protest.

II

PIPPA STOPPED SHORT AND took in the scene around us. "There is still danger."

I nudged Bran. "Come." Tia was already crossing the courtyard below. I gave out orders to every Red Fist within sight. When we reached Feelah in the church, she rose and hugged us.

"No change," she whispered, nodding at Thief.

Pippa reached for a cloth to bathe Thief's head. Far down the hall I could see Bergoin kneeling over a pallet.

I left Father to stand watch. His feet were spread wide and he clutched his staff in both hands. Then I hurried to check on our defenses along the upper walls.

Bran jogged beside me. "Are they safe with just

Father there?" he said. He kept glancing down at the carnage below. His face was whiter than a sea bird.

"I have seen what he can do with that staff," I answered absently, my thoughts grappling with why there were only two Red Fists on the wall. "Take this." I handed Bran my dagger.

Already, I could sense that the Red Fists Marumuk had left behind were not eager to take my orders. Their eyes did not meet mine and they were slow to respond. As the morning approached my uneasiness grew.

The Red Fists stuck to the shadows as if waiting for something else to happen.

"Nothing is right," I muttered to Bran. "The Red Fists are distracted."

"They do not look distracted to me," Bran answered. "We have just come through battle. They are tired."

"Maybe so," I countered. "But we were trained to be at ready, alert to orders, and swift to obey. I do not see this. These Red Fists are waiting for something else to happen."

We made a pass through the tower once again and I stared out into the darkness, where a short time ago the army of Outside had littered the ground. There were still shapes lying on the churned road, likely the bodies of men and horses left for the defenders to bury or burn. But nothing else stirred. The Red Fist posted to watch the road had saluted and reported well.

"At least someone is showing respect!" I muttered to Bran. We returned to the parapet. Below us, families were taking care of their children, fires were being put out, and churchmen ran everywhere with buckets of water.

As we came back toward the tower I pointed at the nearby wall.

"Where are the guards who were posted there?" I grumbled. I looked over my shoulder to the far wall. No Red Fists there either. Several churchmen remained at their posts, looking bewildered and staring down into the courtyard.

"The Red Fists have gone! Listen! There is fighting in the church!" Bran cried.

My stomach sank. The sound of struggling reached us and I wondered why I had not heard it until now.

"Quickly!" I hissed, hurtling past the brothers. The Red Fist watching out the tower window looked up at us questioningly.

"Come, if you are with Marumuk!" I shouted. We took the tower steps down to the courtyard, and I could hear the guard's footsteps behind us.

Rezah suddenly appeared beside me. "Hammoth escaped me!" he cried. "He pretended to guard the rear gates, then came back here."

We sprinted to the church. When I entered the hall, I had to instantly raise my sword, for a weapon came crashing down toward me.

"Father!" I yelled. "It is Coriko!"

Father's eyes were blazing with rage. Blood streamed from an ugly cut on his cheek. He was breathing heavily. All down the length of the great hearths, heads looked up from their pallets. Feelah stood above Thief, wielding the pot that had been used for hot water.

But it was Father's words that made me grow faint. "They have taken my Pippa!" he roared. "And Tia. It was Hammoth."

"Where?" I croaked, hardly able to breathe.

"Through the back gates, just now."

"How many?"

"I counted eight."

"Eight!" Bran groaned.

I stared at the faces in front of me. Father, Feelah, Bran, and Rezah, and one other Red Fist. Hardly enough to take on eight. I ran to the wall and pulled down a bow and quiver, then whirled around to face them. "Who is with me?"

Feelah bent down and kissed her Thief. "I'll be right back," she said to him. "You fight the fever. I'll get the filth who did this to you." She hefted a dagger menacingly.

The guard stood resolutely. Father nodded. Bran slipped a dagger into his belt and took a sword from the wall. Where the remaining Red Fists had gone, I did not know. I could only hope that Marumuk would be on his way back soon.

We ran swiftly across the courtyard, keeping a close watch for any Red Fists who remained. Churchmen stopped working as we passed and several called out encouraging words to Father. So much had happened to their little town in a short time, it was no small wonder there was confusion everywhere we went.

"I did not see which path they took." Father looked cautiously out the main gates to the woods beyond.

"They will go to the harbor," Feelah said. She shifted

her dagger to her other hand. "They must mean to take the hostages by boat."

I nodded. "Yes. Quickly then."

"Why did they take them?" Bran gasped.

"I think that Hammoth took Pippa to get revenge on me. He probably took Tia to make Marumuk do whatever he wants him to do. He uses Marumuk's own plan against him: a hostage to gain power. And that might mean telling Marumuk to honor Hammoth as the new leader of Grassland."

"Is Hammoth as foolish as that?" Father wheezed.

"He thinks of himself more highly than he ought," I answered. My heart sank with every footstep. If they had been prepared enough to take Tia and Pippa, then they would likely launch a boat the moment their feet hit the beach.

Rezah seemed to know my thoughts. "They could not know that Marumuk planned to leave so soon. No way to predict that. Hammoth was waiting for a chance to break away. He took it, the filth!"

There were no words for what I felt. Only one thing gave me cold comfort: Hammoth was being rash, even foolish in his haste. If we hurried, his recklessness would cost him everything he wagered.

"Wings to our feet!" Father looked heavenward. He led us swiftly through the dark woods. The trails had been pounded by thousands of feet over time and were smooth enough for us to run. It was as we drew closer to the water that the roots began to take over and the way became less clear. The smell of brine replaced the dark earth scent of the woods. Father suddenly halted.

"Stop," he commanded. As silence fell we began to listen. I removed my helmet. Voices came from up ahead. Many voices. They spoke quietly, yet with command and urgency.

"It is Marumuk." I pointed to lights off to our right "He is taking Rokhan aboard his ship."

But there were voices in the other direction as well. Father pointed far to the left. "And that is Hammoth."

"How can that be?" Bran asked. "They are no more than two hundred strides apart."

"Perhaps Hammoth uses confusion to make his escape," I said. "He boldly works among the Spears as if he were following commands."

"Boldly?" Rezah answered. "No, foolishly. Hammoth has lost his senses."

Father gripped my arm. "Go to Marumuk. Bring help quickly. I will do what I can to stop them."

"No, Father," I said quietly. "Not this time. You get help. Hammoth will not wait. Tonight he risks all."

I turned to the Red Fist who had come with us. "Take Pippa's father to Marumuk. Tell him that Hammoth is stealing Tia and that you have seen it with your own eyes."

Father sped like a young man with the Red Fist guard right behind him.

"Come, friends," I whispered. Bran, Feelah, and Rezah stole silently behind me as we crept through the last trees to the beach. The gray dawn showed a group of Red Fists sliding their boat to the water's edge. Beside them, only two hundred strides away, Spears were busy loading another craft, unaware that Marumuk's wife was closer than they could have imagined. Feelah started forward, then stopped when I grabbed her arm. I unslung my bow and notched an arrow.

One Red Fist stood leaning on the rope that held the boat to the land. The others seemed to be at their rowing seats. The guard glanced down the beach at the other boats. Then he turned back to the woods and raised his hand.

"Let's go," Feelah whispered.

"Not yet," I answered. "They are waiting." I lowered my bow and pulled out Thief's sword. "And so must we." I looked down the beach. "Hurry, Marumuk," I murmured. I shook my head so that the eyeholes of my helmet gave me clear sight.

"Clever and daring," Rezah whispered. "We must take him down before he reaches the ship."

"There is a danger of harming the girls," I countered. "It must be dagger and sword, no arrows."

A heartbeat later, fifty strides away from us, a small group broke away from the trees and started toward Hammoth's men. There were ten of them. And although the two in the middle wore helmets, their long robes skimming along the sand made them unlikely soldiers. The fact that they were struggling made it even more obvious. But to Marumuk's Spears looking on from farther along the beach, they would seem only as bundles.

"Now!" I cried. Branches snapped and crackled as we tore free of the trees. "Marumuk!" I yelled. I could hear Feelah on one side, panting, and Bran on the other, wheezing as he tried not to trip over his sword. But I did not mind. Pippa was ahead, and Hammoth would not have her.

Three Red Fists charged to meet us, allowing the others to make for the boat. So great was my fury that two of them fell with my downward swing. Even as I lurched to meet the third, Feelah's dagger whistled past my head and crashed into his helmet.

From down the beach I could hear Marumuk's shout. Ripping my cape free, I caught up with Hammoth's group as they entered the water. Two more Red Fists were waiting for me.

I had fought each of them in the Grove at one time or another and beaten them both. They knew it. I threw my cape at their swords, then slashed with my own. Spray soaked me as high as my chest as I rushed past them and into the water. Feelah was yelling with fury and I heard Bran entering the fray. Arrows hit the water.

The girls had been shoved on board. One Red Fist took hold of the rope hanging down from the side of the boat, and swung himself up. Hammoth. The boat rocked with the tide and I could not grasp the rope to go after him. The vessel began to move as the rowers' first stroke broke the waves. I dove for the rope and missed. The boat pulled away.

"Pippa!" I screamed.

Wild splashing came from behind me. Before I could turn, a pair of powerful hands took me by my shoulder and waist.

It was Marumuk. He lifted me out of the water so that my feet dangled in the air. "Ready?"

"Yes!"

"Keep your sword free, for you are about to fly!"

He threw me as Father had thrown the tombstone in the churchyard, and with just as much passion. I caught the stern and my stomach crashed into the hard wooden boards. The planks were slippery with brine and I scrambled wildly for a hold with one hand, hanging onto Thief's sword with the other. An arrow, lodged firmly in the deck, gave me a way up. The Red Fists were crouching down, leaning into their oars. The captives lay on the deck, their hands tied, the helmets removed. Pippa stared up at me.

"Row!" Hammoth screamed. His head shot wildly from side to side as he stood amidships, watching the Spears approach from the beach and using the mast as a shield from arrows. He had not seen me yet. I swung my sword and chopped at the tiller man's arm. He screamed and fell against the steering oar. The boat lurched, pitching me to the deck. Pippa stood up and stumbled to me.

Then Hammoth saw me. "Kill him!" he roared from the prow.

The closest rower pulled a knife. I smacked the tiller in the opposite direction. The sail boom swung and the rower had to duck to keep his seat. I hacked at any other hands that came close. They could not afford to waste time fighting me with Marumuk's ships ready to sail, and I knew it. Already they had lost many men, and they needed the rest to row. Pippa managed to squirm in behind me and pressed herself against the tiller.

Hammoth leapt down.

"Go!" I yelled at Pippa. "Get into the water." She scrambled up to the stern rail. Stepping over Tia, Hammoth charged me. Tia kicked at his feet and he sprawled, landing headfirst among the oarsmen.

Pippa worked her way to her knees, leaning out over the foaming sea. "I will wait for you!" she yelled.

"No!" I dodged a knife. "Get in the water!"

I did not wait to see her splash. In the brief heartbeat I was turned her way, I could see the dragon prow of a Spear ship headed toward us. The oarsmen had seen it too and doubled their efforts.

"Get away while you can!" Tia called to me. Her cheeks were wet with either tears or salt spray, I could not tell. "Go! I will see you again."

Hammoth gained his feet. Two oarsmen joined him.

"I will not leave you," I called to Tia.

"Marumuk comes for me," she answered. "And Pippa is in the water!"

An oarsman kicked me and I spun, falling against the stern.

"Jump, Coriko!"

Hammoth raised his dagger to throw. Taking one last look at Tia, I hurled myself over the edge. Thief's sword disappeared into the sea.

"Corki!" Pippa's voice called.

"I am coming!" Her head bobbed a short distance

away. She lay on her back, desperately trying to keep afloat with her hands tied.

"What about Tia?" Her teeth chattered.

I drew my knife from my belt to cut the ropes. "Hold still, Pippa."

"How can I hold still without sinking?"

"I'm going to cut your hands if you don't stop. Maker, it's cold! There, it's done."

"Look!" Pippa, her hands now free, pointed beside us.

A dragon-prowed ship sailed past us in pursuit of Hammoth. Only a few strokes later, four more ships joined them. A fifth came slowly alongside us.

"Coriko!" I heard Rezah but could not locate him. "All is well?"

"They still have Tia, but she is alive!" There was a splash beside us. A rope suddenly appeared near our heads.

"Bring them aboard!" Rezah shouted.

From the deck, we could see everything. One tall figure stood at the bow of the leading Spear ship. His towering figure looked even more imposing than the dragon head he leaned on.

Hammoth was shouting. "You may have Rokhan, but

we have your wife. It is war, Marumuk! War among the Spears!"

Marumuk made no reply. He leaned forward over the water, his sword drawn. Then he sheathed it. Someone handed him a bow. He waited, riding the waves, holding his target.

Pippa turned away.

Hammoth's taunts were reaching a frenzy. He waved his sword wildly in the air.

"You are a fool, Hammoth," I whispered. "You could have lived in peace."

Suddenly his words ended in a strangled cry. I watched him topple into the rowers. The oars tangled and the ship began to coast.

"Shore!" Rezah called out beside me. Our tiller man heaved to and the prow of our ship turned to the walls of Gotten.

Pippa's soaking hair was sprayed across her cheek.

"I found you," I said.

She nodded.

"And your father is waiting." I pointed to the tall figure standing on the beach.

12

THE SPEAR SHIPS LEFT GOTTEN'S harbor at dawn. Marumuk and Tia stood aboard the flagship with the orange sail stretched to fullness in the wind. It broke my heart to see Bran standing with them. But I understood.

"I will send a ship for you in the summer!" Tia said through her tears. "All of you must come. Plan to stay for many days."

"Many days!" Bran echoed. "I will be better than you with a sword next time you see me, Coriko!"

I could not see his face clearly because of my tears.

Marumuk saluted us.

I raised my hand and kept it high. I waited for Pippa to say a prayer, but she did not speak. When the stern was about to disappear from the harbor I stammered, "Maker keep you and your child in peace."

Pippa nodded, but still said nothing.

"It's cold here, Pippa. Let's go back to the church."

The hearth fires of Gotten, I decided, were warmer than anything else in Pippa's cold country. There were also hot drinks and dry clothes. And everywhere, churchmen hurried to help the wounded, to bring food and blankets.

"Who takes care of *them*?" I asked quietly.

Pippa nodded to one of the Brothers as he poured drink into her cup. She was strangely quiet, staring at the wounded. Once in a while her gaze turned to the room where the churchmen had taken the dead.

The hall was finally quiet. The wounded had been given herbs to help them sleep, and other than the crackling fires, nothing stirred.

I glimpsed Feelah some ways down from us. She had demanded to sleep beside Thief, and Father Bergoin relented, once she promised him that she would get some rest. She slept with her dagger nearby and Thief's hand in hers.

Thief had a fever. He moaned from time to time, but

I took comfort in Father Bergoin's words that he would survive if he made it through to morning.

"Do you think she will be all right?" I whispered.

"Tia?"

"Yes."

Pippa closed her eyes and faced the warming flames. "I do not know." She was quiet again. Then she put her cup down, slid onto her back, and rested her head on my lap. Everything she did these days, even the sound of her moving, made my heart quicken. I leaned over to kiss her.

"No," she said.

"What is wrong? Why are you so quiet? Why would you not pray at the beach? You are acting strangely."

"Children," Father said softly. "Father Bergoin wishes to speak with all of us."

We gathered at the far end of the hearths, where the warmth could still reach us, yet far enough from the injured so as not to disturb them. I could see Thief's pale face from where we stood.

The old churchman sat in a chair against the wall. His face was haggard from tending the wounded. Feelah stood beside me.

"Children," Father Bergoin said. "Most of us have lived to see the new day—a new day without fear of Outside soldiers pillaging our lands. And for that, we thank you." He looked at Pippa. "You held the vision of what could be done when no others could see it." She did not blush as I had expected. Instead, she lowered her head and wept.

"Child?"

"Father," she sobbed, "because of me, many people, children included, lie dead in that room. More lie here, needing healing. Now I cannot pray. I cannot feel."

He closed his eyes and nodded. He reached out to her. When she did not move, I took her small hand and put it into his grasp.

"You feel the burden of true leadership," he whispered. "You seek the good of all, only to find pain and ruin marring the best-laid plans. Evil follows Good and seeks it out, just as the darkness hunts the end of the day."

Pippa looked up at last. "What hope is there?"

"Hope?" The old man smiled. "There is far more than hope. Look at where we stand, child. Not long ago, we had little hope that the walls would still be standing. The army that came here would have wiped out everyone, the whole town." He stared down the line of sleeping wounded. "These will live to see long days ahead. Our gardens will grow and the fields will bring new grain. True leaders feel the weight of their choices. But you must also be able to see the good in the choices you make."

"What good choices?" Pippa murmured.

The old man sighed. "Not all the children escaped your Grassland, did they?"

"No."

"And yet you are here, with some of them. Would you make that same choice again and save *some?*"

Pippa nodded.

"Yes," the old man repeated. "As I would again give my town into the hands of strangers from across the sea if it was the right choice. Tonight I will bury some of my brothers. I will weep by their graves. But I will also rejoice in their sacrifice. For the town of Gotten lives on, and so will they in our memory." He laid a hand on her head. "Be at peace, child. Bear the yoke of leadership well, for it is yours to carry."

He looked at me. "And yours as well. You have much work ahead of you, for I fear you will find your own village in worse repair than this one." Bergoin waved me closer. "Come here, my son."

I stepped up to him. He gripped my arm at the elbow, and his deep-set eyes took command of my own. "You give me hope and faith for our future. For you do not lead with power that comes only from the sword. Rather, you accept guidance from those close to you." He looked at Pippa. "Those who understand that the way of love is better than the path of revenge."

I looked back at Pippa.

"Child." He looked at Feelah. He touched the top of her wild hair briefly. "Your love for your mate is the greatest example to me. I believe that your warrior will be returned to you in good health once his fever breaks." He smiled. "However, he will not enjoy the ride back to your town. It is a bumpy road at best."

She hugged the old man.

"You are all welcome in this place," he said finally. "At any time. Let this be your home to come to whenever you wish."

"Home!" Pippa said out loud. The darkness had left her eyes.

Four days later, the walls of Gotten were far in the distance. We rumbled along the road with loaded carts under the watchful eyes of five churchmen. Father Bergoin had insisted on giving us three horses, an enormous sacrifice so close to planting season.

"They can pull a plow better than a man or woman," he had said. "Bring me a foal or two when you can."

As Father Bergoin had predicted, Thief did not enjoy the ride. He lay on a cart, covered in warm skins, describing each bump with colorful expressions I could not describe to Father.

"That one had something to do with the backside of a horse," I said after Thief's cart took a bad lurch. "I don't know what the other part was."

Father raised a skin filled with Gotten's best ale. "Shall I give him some more?"

One of the Brothers nodded. "Please do."

Pippa had fallen in love with the horses. We had seldom been this close to the animals, and she walked beside them, stroking their warm sides.

I watched her lovingly play with their manes. "I will get you one, if you like." The words slipped out.

223

"You will?"

Her smile made my heart jump.

I dropped back to walk with Father. He rested his arm on my shoulder. "I want to get Pippa a horse," I announced.

His grip tightened just a little. Then he chuckled. "Bergoin is right. There will be foals in time."

I looked up at him.

He winked at me. "And not just horses either, I think. Heaven have mercy!" he bellowed.

I did not understand him, so I changed my thinking. "I am worried about the defense of the village," I said. "Do you not think that we should build a wall, rather than those weak fences? Who knows when the next attack of drunken raiders will come? We should be ready."

He grunted. "*That* is your job, lad. Among many others. For I do not think we will find even our little fences standing."

He was right. When the village came into view, the blackened remains of burned homes glared back at us like the ruined Spear village in Grassland.

"How terrible," Pippa cried.

Villagers broke away from the line as we moved on up the hill to find what was left of their homes.

"They burned the church too," Pippa gasped. When we came to the place where the church had stood so proudly before, only the foundation was left. The roof had burned to tinder, and the giant beams that had held it up lay ruined on the floor in a mess of ash. The pretty window lay in colored pieces. Pippa lifted a small green sliver of glass. "At least we were not in it."

Her father stepped past her and into the ruins. "Coriko, help me."

We stumbled through the ashes and timbers until we reached the center of the floor. I helped him lift away a short beam. The ash wafted about our faces. Father brushed the floor with his foot. Then he got down on his knees and blew away the remaining ash. He felt around with his fingers. After a moment he grunted with satisfaction and pulled. A door lifted and suddenly I was staring down into a cellar, much like the one in which Pippa and I had first taken refuge.

Father stuck his head into the hole and looked about. "Good."

"What is it?" I tried to see past him.

He sat up. "Seed! Enough for a crop we can plant now, to last all winter long. It could be a good year for ale as well." Then his face grew serious. He leaned toward me. "I will need help. This will not happen easily. It will take hundreds of baskets of seed to fill the fields."

I put my hands on my hips. "You forget, Father, that we are used to hard work. If Thief hurries his healing, the planting will be the faster for it. If we were quick at putting shards *in* our baskets, I do not doubt that throwing seed *out* of them will be any harder."

Father raised his eyebrows. "We do not have any homes to live in right now."

I shrugged. "I have lived without one all my life."

He reached over and ruffled my hair. "It is good to have you here, Son."

We made a fire in the center of the old church that night. It would blaze all night to bring comfort—not pain. Thief had gained a little strength now that the journey was over, and he slept soundly. "I owe you a new sword," I whispered.

Someone tugged at my sleeve. "Come with me." Pippa urged me to my feet. I followed her through the graveyard, past the silent stones where her mother lay sleeping, and out to the sandy shore.

A warm wind blew from the south. I picked up a pebble and threw it far into the sea.

"I wonder how long it will take to rebuild this village," I asked, staring at the rolling ocean. "If we work all spring and summer and fall, could homes be ready to live in?"

"I do not mind how long it takes," Pippa answered. "We are *here*. And I have you."

I pulled her along. She gave a happy yelp when we fell to the sand. "Shhh!" I said. "Do you want your father to come running out here?"

She laughed. "No."

I touched her nose. "What do you want then, Pippa? A horse? A house?"

"No."

"What then, green-eyes? What do you wish for?"

As she pulled me down to kiss me, she whispered, "I want *this* place of peace."

ABOUT THE AUTHOR

David Ward was born in Montreal, Quebec, and grew up in the city of Vancouver beside the mountains and ocean. He was an elementary school teacher for eleven years before completing his master's degree. David is currently a writer and university professor in children's literature. He lives in Portland, Oregon, with his wife and three children. This is the third book in a trilogy of Grassland adventures. Visit him online at www.davidward.ca.

THIS BOOK WAS ART DIRECTED and designed by Chad W. Beckerman. The text is set in 12-point Adobe Garamond, a typeface that is based on those created in the sixteenth century by Claude Garamond. Garamond modeled his typefaces on ones created by Venetian printers at the end of the fifteenth century. The modern version used in this book was designed by Robert Slimbach, who studied Garamond's historic typefaces at the Plantin-Moretus Museum in Antwerp, Belgium. The display type is Charlemagne.